A SLOANE MONROE

GONE
DADDY
GONE

CHERYL
BRADSHAW

NEW YORK TIMES BESTSELLING AUTHOR

First US edition April 2017
Copyright © 2017 by Cheryl Bradshaw
Cover Design Copyright 2017 © Indie Designz
All rights reserved.
ISBN: 978-1542386258
ISBN: 154238625X

To my daughter Kylie,
who is and will always be the very best part of me.

"Whatever woman may cast her lot with mine, should any ever do so, it is my intention to do all in my power to make her happy and contented; and there is nothing I can imagine that would make me more unhappy than to fail in the effort."

—Abraham Lincoln

CHAPTER 1

Shelby McCoy walked the same snowy path through the park that she walked every Monday morning after gym class, but today it felt much different than the other times. Something was off, a restlessness causing such unease she stopped for a moment and scanned the area around her. She saw no one, heard no one, yet a discomforting feeling like she was being watched consumed her. Troubled, she kept her eye on her destination and picked up the pace.

The brittle winter air scratched against her skin like sandpaper, chilling her to the core. She pulled the scarf around her neck a bit tighter, burrowed her face into it, and kept going.

Almost there.

Not much farther now.

Just make it past this next turn and everything will be okay.

One week earlier she'd returned to college in Salt Lake City after spending Christmas break at home with her father and his girlfriend in Jackson Hole. The visit had gone well until the end when she confessed to her father that she'd lied to him about her previous semester's grades. She had failed two classes, which, in his eyes, violated their agreement—he would foot the bill as long as she maintained a decent grade point average.

"It's the first semester of the new year, Dad," she had said. "I always bomb at the beginning. Cut me some slack."

"You want slack?" he'd replied. "Fine. When you get back to Utah, go out and get a job. Maybe you should be responsible for payin' your own way from now on."

She had a job—a good one, in fact—but she couldn't talk to him about that either.

The rest of the morning had passed in silence. He didn't speak to her, and she didn't speak to him. When it came time for her to leave, he'd leaned into her car and planted a kiss on her forehead, telling her to drive safely and to text him when she arrived back in Utah. She'd tried apologizing one last time, but he had just swished a hand through the air and walked away. It wasn't the way she'd wanted to leave things, and now she regretted the awkwardness between them.

She lifted a gloved hand and wiped a tear from her eye, thinking about what else she hadn't said when she was back home. She hated college. The only reason she hadn't dropped out was because she knew how disappointed he would be. It didn't matter what she said or how she said it—he wouldn't understand. So what was the point of saying anything at all?

A sound like the cracking of ice startled her back to the present. She slowed down and looked around, again seeing nothing and no one. It was early. The sun hadn't fully risen, and aside from a few park lamps, visibility was poor. Perhaps what she'd heard had been a rabbit or a squirrel. It was possible. Wasn't it? When the noise rang out a third time she froze, staring in the direction the sound had come from—a thicket of trees beside her.

"Hello? Is someone there?"

Silence.

"Hello?"

All was still.

Deciding what she'd heard was nothing more than a tree shaking loose snow from its branches, she shrugged it off and again increased her pace.

"Shelby."

The male voice was faint and low, her name spoken in a whisper.

"Paul, is that you? What, you're stalking me now? Where are you hiding? Come out. This isn't funny."

There was no reply.

"I'm serious, Paul. There's nothing left to say. Please. You have to stop this, okay? You need to leave me alone."

Her instincts kicked in, and she realized the man might have been someone other than Paul. Paul would have presented himself by now, springing out from behind a tree or chucking a snowball in her direction. She slid one of her gloves off and shoved a hand into her pocket, feeling around for the miniature can of mace attached to her keychain. The pepper spray had been a gift from Sloane, her father's girlfriend. When she'd received it, she laughed, thinking Sloane needed to stop being so paranoid about everything. Besides, she was tough and spirited, capable of taking care of herself. She never thought she'd need it, until today.

Now, gripping it in her hand, she was amazed at how much comfort she felt holding the small canister. She pressed it against her chest, her finger on the trigger. If she needed to use it, she'd be ready.

"Shelby McCoy."

This time when she heard her name, she set off into a sprint, only making it a few feet before tripping over a snow-covered rock and plowing face first to the ground. Bruised and in pain, she pushed herself into a kneeling position and whipped around. She saw no one, but her stalker was there, and he was close, the trudge of his footsteps sounding off in the distance.

He's close.

Too close.

Get up, girl.

Get up!

Blood dripped off one of her hands, and her left cheek stung like the side of her face had fallen into a cactus. She had lacerations in multiple places, and the mace keychain was nowhere in sight. Heart thumping inside her chest, she brushed her hands along the snow, searching. *Come on, come on! Where the hell is it?*

Gone.

It was gone.

And she was out of time.

She pounded her fists into the ground and stood. Pulling her cell phone from her pocket, she dialed Maddie. The call went to voicemail, and she remembered Maddie saying she was sleeping over at someone's house the night before, a man she'd been dating. She pressed the end button and dialed again, this time trying her father.

Voicemail.

Again.

Voice trembling, she said, "Dad, please pick up. I need you, Daddy. Please. I'm scared. I think someone's following—"

A gloved hand loomed over her shoulder, ripping the cell phone from her hands. She whipped around, facing the man behind her. He wore a gray beanie, snow goggles, black snow pants, and a jacket, and he was substantial in height, towering over her by at least six inches.

He raised the cell phone above his head, taunting her.

"Give me back my phone, asshole!" she said.

It surprised her when he did what she asked. Then he said, "Call your father one more time. Say goodbye."

This wasn't a random attack. It was calculated. She was the target—his target.

Does he know me?

Does he know my dad?

If only she could sprint for home. But she didn't dare move. He had a pistol pressed against her jacket.

"Go ahead," he said. "Call your father."

She put the phone to her ear and made the call, trying to steady her voice when it went to voicemail yet again. She managed to choke out a few simple words, "I love you, Dad. And I'm sorry. I'm sorry for everything."

Snatching the phone away from her, the man pressed the end button on the phone and then chucked the phone deep into a mass of bushes and trees.

His attention temporarily diverted, she grabbed at his beanie, ripping it off of his head. Though daylight was still minutes away, she caught a glimpse of his thick, brown hair.

Whoever he was, he wasn't familiar.

They stared at one another.

"Who are you? How do you know me?"

"It doesn't matter."

"Maybe not to *you*, but it matters to *me*. I don't understand. Why are you doing this?"

He grabbed her arm, yanking her toward the trees. "Let's go for a walk."

"No! I'm not going anywhere with you."

She tried to pull away, and he swung around, glaring at her.

"Then you'll die. I'll shoot you right here, right now." He rammed the barrel of the pistol into her gut. "Don't make this harder than it has to be, Shelby."

But it *was* hard. She wasn't prepared to die.

Think, Shelby! Do something. Do something now!

She lifted her knee, using all the force she had to drive it right into his crotch. He staggered back, grunting in pain, and she broke free of his grip, running toward Maddie's.

She could see the front porch light from here.

She could get there.

She could make it.

She had to make it.

"Help! Someone help me, please! Please help!"

The crack of gunfire pierced the air, making it come alive again, the bullet connecting, drilling into her back. The force of it jerked her forward. Her legs wobbled beneath her, and she went down. Seconds later, the man was over her again. He grabbed at the hood of her jacket, gagging her as he yanked her behind him. A front door opened in the distance.

Maddie's neighbor, Karen. She stepped out, staring down the path.

Upon seeing her, the man knelt down, pressing the gun to Shelby's forehead. "Not another sound."

He'd get what he wanted, but not because he demanded it. She was in shock, incapable of producing a sound loud enough to carry it where she needed it to go. The neighbor remained outside for a moment and then turned and walked back inside her house.

The impact of the bullet had done its job, and Shelby felt her body shutting down. She blinked through the tears, looking up at the man's unsteady hand like he wasn't sure if he could follow through with shooting her a second time if he had to shoot her again. It was strange. She felt his anger and his rage, but she also felt something else.

Did he feel remorse for what he'd just done?

Through staggered breaths, she said, "I'm dying."

It was an odd thing to say to a stranger who'd just shot her, and she didn't know why she'd said it. Perhaps it was because there was no one else.

He smoothed a gloved hand over her hair. "I know. I'm sorry it had to be this way."

Sorry?

He's sorry?

She wanted to scream, pound her fists into his chest. With what little strength she had left, she reached up, clutching his coat in her hands. "My ... dad ... will find you. You'll pay ... for this."

CHAPTER 2

I'd never been fond of winter, or of snow, or of anything involving frigid, uncomfortable temperatures. So when Cade asked me to spend the weekend with him in a camper in the woods, I was reluctant to go at first. For the past two years, we'd been cohabitating, living together at his home in Wyoming. I still worked as a private investigator, just like I had when I'd lived in Park City, but PI work in Jackson Hole wasn't the same. Jobs were small and mundane. I'd gone from tracking murderers to tracking ignorant people who didn't know how to pay their bills on time, which made me feel like a debt collector. Lately I'd found myself feeling antsy, missing the thrill of the chase, often wondering if the excitement I craved would ever be satisfied again. I loved Cade, but I was restless. I needed a change.

It was morning, and I was sitting on the bed in the master suite of the camper, if one could call a room in a thirty-five-foot vehicle on wheels such a thing. In the corner of the wall, a tiny piece of fake brown paneling about the size of a nickel had ripped out, leaving an irritating black hole behind it. I tried forgetting it was there, but my OCD was on overdrive, demanding I stare at it again and again.

I watched through the small window as Cade attempted to build a fire. He had misplaced the book of matches and was on his knees, hunched over a pile of branches, trying to light kindling the hard way. Minutes passed, and then small bits of smoke turned into a healthy, roaring flame. Proud of his achievement, he slapped a hand on his knee, laughing like Tom Hanks had when he'd created fire in *Castaway*. He looked in my direction to see if I'd noticed, giving me a thumbs-up. On the outside, I was smiling, and proud. On the inside, I dreaded what I knew was coming next: him coaxing me to leave the warmth of the camper and join him.

Lord Berkeley, a.k.a. Boo, my Westie, danced circles around my feet, indicating he too wanted to be outside—now. I scooped him up, pressing my face against his. "Not you too? Do you know how cold it is out there?"

The camper door swung open. Cade walked in, kicked the snow off of his boots, and poked his head around the corner. "Not bad, right? Now I can make you the campfire breakfast I promised."

I smiled. "Looking forward to it."

He pointed at the refrigerator. "There's a plastic bag inside there filled with everything I need. Can you hand it to me?"

I wrapped my blanket around me, walked to the refrigerator, and retrieved the bag, handing it to him.

He leaned in and we kissed. "Can't believe you won't part with the blanket. With the generator going, it's eighty degrees in here at least. I'm roastin' to death. Aren't you?"

I grinned. "Nope. Not yet."

"There's nothin' like a good breakfast cooked over a campfire. Wanna come hang out with me while I cook?"

There it was—the wind up and the pitch.

"It's only twenty-five degrees outside, isn't it?"

He pushed the door back open, looking at a temperature gauge on the side of the camper. "It's ... uhh ... well ... it's a bit on the cold side. Not too bad."

"How cold are we talking?"

"Twenty-one. Sun's out though. If you bring the blanket and I stoke up the fire, you won't even notice."

Oh, I'd notice, but he seemed determined, and I didn't have the heart to refuse him. I laced up my snow boots, grabbed a beanie, pushed it over my short, black hair, and followed him outside. He pulled a camp chair close to the fire, and I sat down, tucking Boo beneath the layers of blanket on my lap.

Cade dumped a bowl of shredded potatoes into the pan, added an entire stick of butter, and then stood up, breathing in a lungful of crisp, mountain air. "It's beautiful up here, isn't it? I suppose if I lived somewhere else, I could always come back and visit."

Somewhere else?

"You don't live somewhere else though. You live here."

"I was hopin' we could talk about that. It's one of the reasons I wanted to come up here this weekend."

I was curious to know what he was getting at.

"Okay, let's talk."

"I've been thinkin' about puttin' my house up for sale and leavin' this place."

The announcement took me by surprise. He'd always seemed content in Jackson Hole, and I never thought he'd leave. "How long have you been thinking about moving?"

"A few months now."

"What about your job? You're the chief of police. You can't just walk away."

"Why not? My tenure's almost up. I knew the job would only be for a few years when I accepted it."

"Why do you want to move?"

He took the lid off the pot, stirred the potatoes, added a bit of seasoning, and put the lid back on again. "There's a lot more to life than spendin' all of it in one place."

I agreed.

"Plus, I've never thought you were happy here, and truth be told, I don't know if I am either."

"I haven't complained since I've been here, have I? I'm fine."

"Fine isn't good though. It's gettin' by. You're here because I'm here, and I don't need to be here anymore. Shelby's in college and livin' on her own now. Why not find a place we both like and go there together?"

"Are you serious?"

"'Course. I wouldn't bring it up otherwise."

He grinned at me in a way that reminded me of the first time we met, when I had to do a double take to convince myself Brad Paisley hadn't just entered the room. "What do you think?"

I shook my head. "I won't let you give all of this up for me, if that's what you're doing. I thought you loved it here."

He raised a brow. "I *like* it here. Let's not get crazy."

"Where would you go? Have you thought about it?"

"You mean where would *we* go? I don't know. Figured we could decide together. If you could live anywhere, where would it be?"

It was a loaded question, one I hadn't considered for a long time. "I'm not sure. I need time to think about it."

"You should, think about it."

I smiled. "I will."

For several minutes, I daydreamed about where I'd go, the wheels of opportunity spinning 'round and 'round inside my head. I liked our life together, and Jackson Hole was beautiful, breathtaking even. But he was right. It wasn't me, and it never would be.

Cade glanced inside the plastic bag and frowned.

"What's wrong?" I asked.

"I thought I brought silverware out here when I grabbed the plates. Guess I didn't."

I looked down at Boo. Even tucked inside the blanket, he was shivering. "I think the furry one is ready to go back inside. I'll get them."

I was in and out in less than a minute. When I returned with the silverware in hand, Cade offered me a plate. I eyeballed it, noticing he had added a little something extra next to the scrambled eggs, potatoes, and bacon. A pebble. And not just any pebble. A pebble shaped like a heart.

I picked it up, smoothing it in my hand. "This is so sweet. Where did you find it?"

"Wasn't easy, but I did. Do you know how male penguins woo a mate?"

I shook my head.

"When the male finds a female he wants to be with for life, he searches the beach for the perfect pebble," he said. "Then he offers it to the female. If she accepts it, they remain together for the rest of their lives."

He bent to one knee, and it all made sense—the comment about moving, why we were really there, the pebble. He grabbed my hand, rubbing his thumb along my palm, and reached into his coat pocket, pulling out a black velvet box. Popping it open, he held it out in front of me. "Remember the night we first met at the bar downtown? I asked if you wanted to dance, and you corrected my grammar. I remember lookin' into your eyes and thinkin' you were the kind of girl I'd go through hell and back to find—the one I never thought existed. These past few years with you have been the best of my life. I never knew I could love a woman the way I love you. When I wake up each mornin' and see you layin' by my side, all I want is to get through my day so I can come back to you again."

"Cade, I—"

He squeezed my hand. "Just hang on a second, let me finish. I haven't just been thinkin' a lot about movin' lately. I've been thinkin' about us, about our future together, and the only future I see is one with you in it. Sloane Monroe, will you marry me?"

A multitude of feelings surged through me. I was stunned, and happy, and caught off guard. I'd prepared for this moment, sure one day it would come. And yet, here it was when I least expected it. After marrying once before when I was way too young, I'd sworn off ever marrying again. Until now. Until him.

"Well," he said. "Whaddya say?"

Before I could say anything, I became distracted by the sound of a vehicle tearing up the road at great speed. It turned in our direction, jerking to an abrupt stop. "Hey, umm, I think someone's here."

Cade's eyes were still focused on me, as if he hadn't heard a thing. Then he turned, looking distraught. His perfect moment had been spoiled. He released my hand, shook his head, and stood, trying to get a good look at the people in the truck's cab. "Who in the hell would be comin' into our camp right now?"

I shrugged. "Who else knows we're here?"

The truck's passenger-side door opened, and Cade's feisty Aunt Bonnie hopped out. She didn't look like the spirited woman I was used to seeing. She looked weary and forlorn. Something wasn't right.

"Bonnie?" Cade said. "Your timing is the worst. What are you doing here?"

She approached us, glanced down at the ring box Cade had snapped shut, and blotted her eyes with a tissue. "I'm sorry to disturb you two, especially now when you were ... well, it looks like you were ... anyway, I didn't have a choice. The two of you need to come home right now."

"Why?" Cade asked. "What's happened?"

More tears, and then, "It's Shelby, Cade."

"What do you mean? Did she call you? Is she all right?"

The driver's-side door of the truck opened, and Bonnie's boyfriend Hank walked toward us. He was bald, had a thick beard, and was muscular for a man in his upper sixties. Hank slung his arm around Bonnie. "Would you like me to do it, dear?"

Bonnie shook her head. "No, Hank. It's all right. It needs to come from me."

"What's going on with Shelby?" Cade asked.

"Sloane's friend Maddie called me this morning," Bonnie said. "She's been trying to get in touch with the two of you for several hours."

"We don't have any cell service out here," I said. "Did Maddie say why?"

Seconds passed in silence, and it seemed Bonnie couldn't bring herself to say what needed to be said. She deferred to Hank. "I thought I could do it, but I ... I just can't."

"Bonnie, please," Cade said. "You're the toughest woman I know. To see you like this ... it's makin' me worry."

"I'm so sorry, Cade. I wish I didn't have to be the one to tell you. Shelby was walking home from school and she was attacked."

"Attacked how?"

"Someone shot her."

A frantic Cade grabbed Bonnie's arms. "What are you sayin', Bonnie? Who attacked her? Why?!"

"I don't know yet. No one does. Maddie is working with the police to piece together what happened."

Cade reached in his pocket and pulled out his keys. "We'll leave the camper here and head down. Where did the bullet hit her, and which hospital is she at?"

Hands on hips, Bonnie bent toward the ground and let the tears flow. "She's not at the hospital. She didn't survive. Our sweet girl is gone, Cade. She's gone."

CHAPTER 3

After convincing Cade it wasn't the best time for him to be driving, I grabbed Boo from inside the camper and decided everything else could remain until later. The four of us piled into Hank's truck and headed for Utah. It was a quiet ride at first, and my thoughts turned to the last visit we'd had with Shelby the week before, nitpicking details I remembered, anything that seemed unusual or off somehow. The visit had been peculiar—the same Shelby we were used to seeing, but in different packaging. She had arrived carrying an expensive Gucci handbag and wearing large, round diamond earrings—and they didn't look like cubic zirconias to me; they looked like the real deal. When I had inquired about how a poor college student with no job could afford such high-end items, she blew me off, saying the diamonds were fake and the handbag and the boots were borrowed. The explanation seemed logical, but thinking about it now, I realized I'd never really bought it.

Cade reached out, tapping Bonnie on the shoulder. "I need you to tell me everything you know so far."

"Maddie didn't say a lot over the phone. She was in a rush. She wanted to talk to you first."

"Yeah, well, my phone still doesn't have service, so I feel like I'm sittin' here spinnin' my wheels until I can get on the phone."

"I'm doing my best to get you there as fast as I can," Hank said. "Once I hit the highway, I'll do ninety. Should be able to shave an hour off our trip if we don't run into any traffic."

Cade patted him on the back. "Thanks, Hank. I appreciate it."

Bonnie faced Cade. "I'll tell you what I do know. Maddie's neighbor called her this morning after she heard gunfire in the park next to the cul-de-sac they live on. I guess Maddie wasn't home at the time. Maddie told the neighbor Shelby had called her, but she'd missed her call. She tried calling back, and Shelby didn't answer. Maddie drove home to see what all the fuss was about. By the time she arrived, the police were there, and they told her they had found Shelby in the park."

"What do you mean they *found* her?"

Bonnie shook her head. "I don't know, Cade. Maddie said Shelby had an early morning class each Monday and a three-hour break before the next one. Instead of staying at school, she usually walked back to Maddie's guesthouse."

"Why was she walkin' in the first place? Where was her car?"

"In the shop being repaired. I'm not sure why."

"She told me she walked to her morning classes sometimes," I said. "She liked how quiet it was in the park."

"Why are the police saying she was attacked?" Cade asked. "Aside from the bullet wound, do they have proof of an attack? Did the neighbor see anything?"

"I don't think so. Shelby has cuts on her face and hands."

"How many times was she shot?"

"Once."

"Where?"

Bonnie's shifted her gaze from Cade to the snow-covered mountains out the window.

"Where was she shot, Bonnie?" Cade asked again.

"In the back," Bonnie whispered.

He gritted his teeth. "Are you kiddin' me? What kind of … who would do somethin' like that?!"

"I don't know anything more than what I just said. I'm sorry. Maddie told me to tell you she'd explain more when she sees you, and she'll examine Shelby as soon as she has permission."

My phone made several dinging sounds. Cade's followed. We had service. Cade picked his phone out of his pocket and stared at the screen. "Looks like I have a few voicemail messages."

He put the phone on speaker, and we listened to a terror-stricken Shelby, in what I assumed were the final moments of her life. "Dad, please pick up. I need you, Daddy. Please. I'm scared. I think someone's following—"

There was a pause, followed by Shelby cursing. A muffled voice was heard in the background, a voice not belonging to Shelby. The voice was deep and low, a man's. His words were broken and choppy, too hard to translate. Once he stopped talking, the line went dead.

Cade made a fist, thrusting it into the seat multiple times before burying his head in his hands. "I should have never sent her back! I should have never let her leave without fixin' things between us first!"

I knew nothing I could say would soothe him, but I had to try.

"None of this is your fault," I said.

"'Course it is. Before she left, she tried smoothin' things over, tried to make peace, and I rejected her. She died thinkin' I let her down. Can you imagine? In her final moments, she called and I didn't answer. She must have thought I didn't want to talk to her. The moment she needed me most, I wasn't there. I let her down, and I'll never forgive myself for that."

CHAPTER 4

Maddie's long, blond pigtails bounced up and down as she speed-walked toward me. She enveloped me in her arms, pulling me close. I choked back the tears I'd so bravely kept at bay, trying to remain calm while the sea of turmoil swirled around me. She was my oldest friend, my closest confidant, the one person who could read me better than anyone.

"Let it out, Sloane," she said. "It's okay."

"I can't. I need to be strong for Cade."

"Cade will understand. How's he holding up?"

I broke from our embrace and glanced back, ensuring he wasn't within earshot. He stood at the door of Maddie's lab with a cell phone to his ear, breaking the news about Shelby to Wendy, Shelby's mother and his drug-addicted, unstable ex-wife.

"He's not good," I said. "Although I keep waiting for him to explode. It's coming."

"He's in shock right now. We all are."

"There's more to it. He's struggling with the guilt he feels over what happened the last time Shelby visited. They fought over her grades. It didn't end well. He can't stop replaying it in his mind."

"Yeah, I knew things were off between them," Maddie said. "Shelby talked to me about it when she returned last week. You know she wanted to quit school, right?"

I crossed my arms, nodded. "The day before she left, we had a nice talk. I told her I thought she should remain in school for one more semester. Her first year of college was rough. She didn't like living on campus. When you invited her to stay at your guesthouse this year, she was ecstatic. I was hoping it would give her the boost she needed to stay."

"I dunno. She seemed to think she didn't need school to live the kind of life she wanted, and she acted like she didn't need her dad's money either. She told me there were other ways she could take care of herself."

"Other ways? How?"

Maddie shrugged. "I dunno. When I pressed her on it, she clammed up."

Cade ended his call and walked over.

"How did it go with Wendy?" I asked.

"'Bout the same as it always goes. She's gonna head this way tomorrow. I tried holding her off, but you know how she is. With all that's goin' on, I can't deal with her right now."

"Where is she living these days?" I asked.

"Says she's with some new guy in Michigan."

Cade turned toward Maddie. "I want to know everything. How close are the police to catching the piece of trash responsible for Shelby's murder?"

"We're all working as fast as we can, Cade. Believe me. So far we can't find anyone who saw anything. I wish we knew who did it. I'd kill him myself."

"She's been living in your guesthouse for four months," Cade said. "You must have seen kids come and go, met some of her friends. You know the people we should be talkin' to, right? I want names."

"Shelby hardly ever invited anyone over. She was gone a lot. The guesthouse is small. I figured she preferred hanging out somewhere bigger, where she could be with all of her friends."

"Did she say anything about having any problems with anyone lately?"

Maddie shook her head. "She got along with everyone. Well, everyone except Paul."

Cade raised a brow. "Who is Paul?"

I gave Maddie a hard stare, knowing she'd interpret the stare's specific meaning. Cade didn't know about Paul, not that it mattered now. Whatever secrets Shelby kept, they all needed to come out.

"Paul's ahh ... someone Shelby had been hanging out with, I guess." Maddie said. "Never met the guy though."

"Hangin' out?" Cade asked. "Friends or more than friends?"

"Well, I guess *hanging out* wouldn't be the right choice of words."

"What are the right words?"

"Paul was Shelby's ex-boyfriend," Maddie said. "I think he was, at least."

Cade raised brow. "Boyfriend? Since when?"

"I don't know. She only mentioned him to me a couple of times. She said he was someone she was dating, and then maybe three or four weeks ago, she said they broke up."

"What's his last name?"

Maddie shrugged. "I don't know. I didn't ask. Shelby was always private about her personal life, so I never pushed."

He whipped around, gauging my reaction. "Why don't you look surprised? Did you know about this guy too?"

This wasn't a conversation I wanted to be having right now. "She mentioned him to me a few weeks ago, but it's like Maddie said, I didn't think much about him, especially since she said they broke up."

"Any guy datin' my daughter is a guy I deserved to know about, no matter how insignificant. You hid it from me."

"I didn't *hide* anything."

"Yeah, you did. Since when do we have secrets from each other? I thought you trusted me. Guess you don't."

There it was—the anger I knew would come—finally pushing its way to the surface. The insult stung like a slap to the face. Any other day I would have clapped back. But he was feeling helpless, like a father who'd failed to protect his daughter. Right now he needed someone to blame, and I was it. "It wasn't my intention to keep it from you. She told me they had dated for a while and then said they broke up. Since he wasn't relevant in her life anymore, I didn't think it mattered."

I could have said anything. He wouldn't understand.

"Why was she so afraid to tell me about the guys she was datin'? She's dated guys in the past I haven't liked. How was this one any different?"

"If he wasn't someone she was serious about, she probably assumed there was no point in bringing him up to you."

"Why did they break up?" Cade asked.

"I don't know," Maddie said. "The only thing Shelby said was that he was too clingy. She did mention Paul hadn't taken the breakup well, but I never got the impression she was concerned for her safety or worried in any way. She acted like he was more of a nuisance than anything else. I suspected the breakup had something to do with Jesse."

Cade threw his hands in the air. "Who the hell is Jesse?"

"He was another boy she'd started seeing," Maddie said. "I don't know much about him either."

Cade looked at me. "Did you know about Jesse too?"

"When Shelby came home this last time, she said she had gone out with Jesse a few times. It seemed like they were just getting to know each other."

"Maddie, do the police know about these guys?" Cade asked.

Maddie nodded. "They know everything I know."

"There must be photos of these guys somewhere—in her house, on the Internet—somewhere."

"I've never seen any," Maddie said. "I even asked her to show me. She kept saying she would, but she never did."

He pointed to the lab door. "I want to see her."

Maddie placed a hand on Cade's shoulder. "Being chief of police, I know you've inspected bodies before, but this is different. She's not some Jane Doe you don't know. It won't be easy."

"Don't care," he said. "No matter how hard it is, I still have to do it."

CHAPTER 5

I focused on the sound of my shoes squeaking along the rubbery, blue floor of the lab. It helped divert my attention away from why we were there. When we were halfway through the room, Maddie came to an abrupt stop, and it became eerily quiet. I'd been in that exact lab many times over the years, but today it felt different, almost sacred, like if I raised my voice above a whisper, it would be a sign of disrespect.

Three polished metal tables were positioned in the far corner of the room. The first two were empty. A sheet covered a body on the third. I assumed it was Shelby.

"I'll lift the sheet off and give you a few minutes," Maddie said. "Then I'll cover her back up, and we can talk about what I've learned so far, okay?"

Cade and I nodded, and the three of us approached the table. I grabbed Cade's hand. My lungs felt tight and heavy, constricted, and I struggled for breath.

Maddie folded the sheet down with the gentlest of movements. Cade glanced at his daughter, blinking through the tears that couldn't be stopped.

His voice shaky, he reached for Shelby's hand. "She's so cold. So cold and pale."

I gazed upon Shelby's face and the reality of the situation hit me, spiraling me down the rabbit hole, my body limp and weak like I was made of air. My hand slipped out of Cade's, and I gripped the side of the table, trying to keep myself from going down.

"Sloane," Maddie said. "What's going on? Are you okay?"

"I can't ... it's just, seeing her like this ... I'm not ... I don't think I was ready for ..."

Maddie covered Shelby back up and walked around the table, pressing her hands into the sides of my face. "Look at me, Sloane. Look at me. Forget about everything else and focus on the sound of my voice for a minute."

"What's goin' on, Sloane?" Cade asked.

"She's having an anxiety attack," Maddie said. "You know this happens sometimes, right?"

"I mean, yeah, I do. She hasn't had one in a while."

I hadn't had one because life in Jackson Hole was simplistic, nothing stimulating enough to push my nerves to the surface. It had been so long since my last episode, I thought I'd moved past having them anymore. Now I realized I'd been fooling myself.

"Sloane is usually good at managing her anxiety most of the time. She hides it well too." Maddie pointed to a cabinet across the room. "Grab a glass out of the cabinet and get her some water, will you?"

Cade nodded and walked away.

"Sloane, listen to me," Maddie said. "I need you to breathe."

I shook my head. "It's just hard. I feel like I can't get any air in."

"Yes, you can. We'll do it together—deep breath in, deep breath out. Good. Two more times."

Cade returned with the water. Maddie instructed him to grab a chair from her desk and bring it over. He did, and I sat down, feeling embarrassed, watching the two of them hover over me like *I* was the wounded bird. This wasn't about me, and yet here I was taking the focus away from the precious moments Cade needed with his daughter. I was better than this. And even if I wasn't, I had to be.

I sipped the water and stabilized my breathing. "I'm so sorry, Cade. I didn't mean for that to happen."

He cupped my chin in his hand. "Hey, don't worry about it, okay? You loved her too. She was a big part of your life. You were more of a mother to her than her own mother, and she loved you for it."

A mother.

I felt elated and brimming with sorrow at the same time.

Maddie touched my shoulder. "You feeling better now?"

I nodded. "Let's try again."

"Do you think you can handle it this time?"

"Of course. Go ahead."

Maddie returned to Shelby, lifting the side of the sheet up, focusing on Shelby's hands. "She has fresh cuts on both hands, and I believe these came from her having fallen."

"How do you know that?" Cade asked.

"When I inspected the crime scene, I found blood next to a rock along the path she walked this morning. I took a sample. I'm sure it's hers, which would explain the cuts on her hands. My guess? She fell and scraped them against the rock, trying to break her fall."

"What else did you find?" Cade asked.

"Two sets of footprints in the snow. Her boots left a consistent pattern. It was early in the morning, and the path hadn't had much foot traffic yet, so I could see where she entered the park and how far she went before her shoe pattern became more spread out. At first she was walking, and about three quarters of the way, it looks like she started running. I believe she fell, and her assailant caught up to her."

"The second set of prints," I whispered.

"Exactly. He attempted to smear them, but it was dark, and he missed a few."

"You say the assailant was a he," Cade said, "which is exactly what we heard in the background when Shelby …" He choked on his words, unable to continue.

I jumped in to explain. "Shelby called and left a message on Cade's phone, apparently just as she was attacked. We could hear a man's voice in the background before the phone cut off."

"I didn't know about the phone call. How horrible for you." Maddie paused, pursing her lips. She took a deep breath in and continued. "So yes, the prints look to be of a male wearing boots. I had a few casts made, and I'll be analyzing those today. From the position of the prints, it's my opinion that he caught up to her, and there was a struggle. She must have found a way to break free, because more of her prints were found a little farther along. It looks like she was running away when he shot her."

Cade ran a hand down Shelby's hair. He bent down, kissing her forehead, pausing a moment before standing up again. "Were you able to determine where he went after she was shot?"

"We followed his prints past the pond and into the parking lot. They disappeared after that, leading me to believe he got into a vehicle and drove away."

"Talk to me about how she was shot."

Maddie nodded. "The way the bullet entered her body is consistent with a person who had been running, and based on the trajectory, I believe he was at least four feet behind her when he fired. The bullet entered her back, pierced her lung, and continued through her heart."

"It happened before it was light out. How did he get such a good shot off?"

"The park has a few streetlamps. I found additional blood right below one of them. He could have aimed, waited for her to come into the light, and then shot her."

"Was the bullet a through-and-through?"

Maddie shook her head. "It's intact though. I extracted it before you arrived. My assistant is running tests now. I have photos. If you're interested, I'll show you."

Cade nodded.

Maddie grabbed a folder off of her desk, riffled through a series of shots, and pulled one out. "Take a look."

Cade leaned over Maddie's shoulder, his eyes focused on an enlarged bullet. "Looks like a forty to me."

"Yep. It is. A Speer Gold Dot Centerfire."

"Where was she when you found her?"

"She had been moved to the side of the path," Maddie

said. "She was face up in the snow. Her hands rested on her lap, one over the other."

"Like she'd been positioned?"

"You ask me, the way her arms were crossed was almost more of a sign of respect. He could have shot her and taken off, leaving her where she fell. He didn't."

Maddie set the folder down, grabbed the sheet, and covered Shelby back up again. Cade stared as if in a trance, his eyes reflecting the pain he had tried his best to hide.

"Is there … uhh … anything else I should know?" he asked.

"There is *one* thing. Tucked beneath her hands, I found a playing card, a Ten of Hearts."

Cade and I exchanged glances, confused.

"What in the hell is that supposed to mean?" he asked.

"You probably want to talk to the guys working the case, get their take on it. I was just asked to process the card for prints. There is something else I should tell you."

"Yeah?"

"Written on the card, it said: *How does it feel?*"

"How does *what* feel?"

Maddie shrugged. "Who knows? Nothing else was written on it."

"Did you find any prints on the card?"

She shook her head. "It was clean."

"Anything else?"

"Her cell phone was found about thirty feet away from her body, in between a few trees, broken. I pulled one solid print off the back side and one partial off the front. Both were Shelby's. I assume the killer wore gloves."

"Who's running the show over at the police department

now?" I asked. "I heard they were putting in a new chief of police. Is he anyone I know?"

Maddie looked away. "It's ... umm ... well ... yeah. You could say it's someone you know."

"Why are you stalling? Just tell me who it is."

"You're not going to like it."

"Why? How bad can it be?"

Judging by the look on her face, I had cause to worry.

"You may as well tell me," I said. "I'd like to drop in, let him know I'm around, and plan on being a part of this case."

She bit the side of her lower lip. "I understand. It's just you're not going to like talking to the new chief, Sloane, and he's not going to like talking to you. I've been meaning to tell you and just hadn't yet."

"So tell me."

"The new chief of police is Coop."

CHAPTER 6

Drake Cooper, who went by the nickname Coop, was a former Park City detective and a man who had salted every wound on every case I'd worked on when I lived there. He had also saved my life on one occasion. Not because he wanted to and not because he liked me. He didn't.

I had been sitting with Cade outside of Coop's office for the last half hour, waiting for him to return from a meeting. Cade hadn't uttered a word since we sat down. He'd leaned back in the chair and crossed one boot over the other, staring at the wall like it was playing a movie. I didn't blame him for checking out. I wanted to do the same.

I rested a hand on his leg. "How are you doing?"

He remained focused on the wall. "Can we talk about what happened earlier?"

"Sure."

I assumed he meant Shelby. I was wrong.

"We have never talked much about your panic attacks. I mean, we have, but not in depth. I'm thinkin' we should. Maddie knew what to do when it happened, and I didn't."

He was deflecting, choosing a topic he had the ability to discuss instead of the one he didn't.

"What do you want to know?"

"How many years have you had them?"

I shrugged. "It's hard to say. They've been happening for a long time."

"Do you recall the first one you had?"

"The first one I remember was when I was a kid. I remember a strange feeling of panic and fear hitting me at once. It was like this horrible pit in my stomach that wouldn't go away. At the time I didn't understand what was happening or why."

"What caused it?"

What had always caused them, my parents, every time their arguments escalated into a yelling match. I handled it by seeking shelter in my room, curling myself into a ball on my bed. It was my safety, my impenetrable bubble.

"I've talked to you about the way my dad treated my mom," I said.

"Yeah, I remember."

"The nights he lost control, I'd hide under my covers in bed, struggling to breathe. I think the anxiety attacks first started over the guilt I felt."

"You were a child. What did you have to feel guilty about?"

"I couldn't protect my mother from my father, from his explosive rants. I was too young. I'd close my eyes and pretend I was older and stronger. I pictured myself helping her, even though I couldn't."

"Your childhood was so long ago. All these years later and your anxiety attacks haven't gone away?"

"They come and go. We've been together long enough for you to see they're not frequent. Stressful situations trigger it. Most of the time I can manage it. Sometimes I can't."

"It explains why you grew up to be a private investigator, and why you prefer to take on the more dangerous cases."

I shrugged. "I guess. Having a grandfather in the FBI also fostered my interest. He used to talk to me about his job, and I wanted to grow up to be just like him."

Cade glanced down the hallway. "So, what's the deal with this Coop guy?"

"What do you mean?"

"How hard is it gonna be to work with him?"

Hard.

Borderline impossible.

But I knew I shouldn't say that, so I didn't.

"You've met him. You remember what he was like. It would be better if you let me do the talking when he gets here, okay?"

"I remember when he helped you find Shawn Hurtwick, the guy who nabbed Shelby a while back. He seemed like an okay guy to me then."

I crossed my arms in front of me. "Coop's better with men than women. We have history, and it's not good."

"What kind of history are we talkin' about?"

"He doesn't respect what I do for a living. When I lived in Park City, he always thought I got in the way of his investigations, even though I managed to help him with every case he had that I'd been hired to work on."

He raised a brow. "If things aren't good between the two of you, I should talk to him."

"I know how to handle him, and I know what sets him off."

Coop's oversized, oval-shaped head rounded the corner, heading in our direction. He passed us without making eye contact, stepped into his office, and closed the door, even though it was obvious by the disgusted look on his face that he knew I was there.

And so it begins.

I did a knock-and-walk, entering his office without waiting for him to summon me in first. Cade followed. The familiar scent of Old Spice saturated the room. I lifted a hand to my mouth and coughed to keep from gagging. "Hey, Coop. Long time."

"Yep."

He kept his eyes glued to a stack of paperwork on his desk, still refusing to acknowledge me.

"I need to talk to you," I said.

"Yep, I'm aware."

"We've been waiting for almost an hour."

"Aware of that too."

I plopped down on a chair. Cade did the same.

"Ignoring me isn't going to work," I said. "We're talking to you whether you like it or not."

He looked at me and grinned. "Well, well. There's the bratty girl I remember."

And there was the asshole *I* remembered.

Cade held a hand out to Coop. "I'm Cade McCoy, Shelby McCoy's father."

Coop glanced at Cade's outstretched hand and did nothing. "Yep, I remember you."

"We would like to know what's going on with Shelby's case so far," I said.

"Oh, would you? And you just thought you'd come on down here and I'd spill it all because it's personal, right? You just came from seeing your gal pal at the lab. I'm sure she told you more than you need to know."

"Everything Maddie knows isn't everything *you* know though, is it?" I said.

Coop tapped his big, fat thumb on the edge of the desk. "I'm not sharing anything with you, sweetheart. I'll do everything I can to catch the guy, just like I always do."

"So will we," Cade said.

Coop sighed, turned toward Cade. "Sorry about what happened to your kid. It's a harsh world out there, and it sucks. But I don't want you here. I don't have time to babysit you. Either one of you."

"I've never asked you to," I said.

Cade leaned forward, pressing a finger on the desk to emphasize his next words. "I don't think you understand. This is my daughter we're talkin' about. I'm the chief of police in Jackson Hole, which I'm sure you know. I'm not just some guy off the street who doesn't have a clue what he's doin'. If you refuse to talk to me or work with me, it won't change a thing. I'll find the guy myself."

Coop leaned back in his chair. "My new lead detective is out of town. He's been apprised of the situation and is headed back now. I've asked him to sit down with you both when he returns to see if you have any information that will help us identify your daughter's killer. Then I want you to go home.

The last thing I need right now is an overzealous father hindering my investigation."

"I'm not leavin'," Cade said.

"Suit yourself. But if I see you around, interfering with my case, I'll have you arrested. You think you're some Wyoming big shot, and you're not. You're in Utah now, and *I* run the show around here."

Cade slammed his fist onto the desk. "If you knew what it was like to lose a kid, maybe you'd have a bit more decency and wouldn't be such a prick."

Coop's eyes narrowed, and I prepared myself for the reply I knew was coming.

"My daughter was shot and killed in the line of duty," Coop said, "so don't *ever* come into my office talking to me about loss like I don't know what it is. Now get up and get the hell out of my office."

CHAPTER 7

An exhilarating feeling pulsed through the man as he tapped on the window with the tip of his fingernail. He'd tap four or five times and then stop, just enough to make Sloane and Cade stir in bed, but never enough to make either of them suspect he was standing there, looming outside the bedroom window of Maddie's house, watching them sleep.

He risked exposure this way, but he didn't care.

Besides, he liked it.

He liked it a lot.

He envisioned doing a lot more than standing idly by, merely taunting them. He envisioned killing them while they slept. He'd even pressed the barrel of his gun against the window, thinking of how easy it would be to murder them both right there in bed. But the timing wasn't right, and neither was the order, even though picking off two birds with two bullets at once would definitely be efficient. But he failed to see the satisfaction of finishing what he'd started tonight. It was premature. Better to hold off and wait for more opportune moments. He needed to be patient, even though he didn't want to be.

Today had been a good day. He'd watched Cade and Sloane arrive, witnessing the hurt on their faces as they joined with friends and law enforcement to mourn the passing of Shelby.

Shelby.

He had to admit he'd felt badly when he shot her, a sense of regret, her last words playing over and over in his mind. But it had to be done. A point had to be made, and she was the perfect one to make it. They had all been blindsided, just like he had been blindsided a short time ago.

One down.

Four to go until I'm finished.

Sloane tossed and turned in the bed, and just as he raised a finger to toy with her again, headlights beamed in the distance, a car driving up Maddie's road and turning toward the house. It was unexpected. Who would be visiting at this hour? He pulled the top of his hoodie over his head, glancing once more through the window before disappearing into the night.

Sleep tight, everyone.

I'll be coming for you all soon.

CHAPTER 8

A tapping sound like hail pelting glass woke me from a dream so real I saw myself living Shelby's final moments like I was there with her, watching the murder happen in front of me. I jolted up in bed and looked at the time. It was four o'clock in the morning, and I knew I wouldn't be able to go back to sleep again. Not now.

I glanced out the window. It was a clear night. No wind. No breeze. So what was the noise I'd just heard? I waited and listened, wondering if I would hear it again. The house went quiet for a time, and then the tapping started up again.

Cade rolled over and ran a hand down my back. "You havin' trouble sleepin'?"

"Yeah."

"It's all right. I can't sleep either."

"I keep hearing something, a noise."

"Coming from where?"

"Outside, I think."

He pushed the blanket to the side, grabbing his pistol off the nightstand. "Stay here. I'll take a look around."

Not okay with being left behind, I stood, following him to the next room. He switched the porch light on, cracked the door a few inches, and looked out, pulling it all the way open once he saw who was standing on the other side—a young girl about Shelby's age wearing a coat, a pair of yoga pants, and UGG boots. She had curly, auburn hair that she'd pulled into a messy bun, and she wore dark ruby-colored lipstick, which seemed a bit odd considering the hour.

"Can I help you?" Cade asked.

"I'm looking for Shelby's parents."

"I'm her father."

She looked past him at me. "You're Sloane, right?"

I nodded. "Who are you?"

"Veronica. Shelby's friend."

Curious. Shelby had never mentioned anyone named Veronica to me before. "Veronica what?"

She shook her head. "It doesn't matter. Can I come in for a minute?"

Cade stepped back, allowing her inside.

"How do you know Shelby?" I asked. "From school?"

She stuck her hands inside her coat pockets. "Umm ... not exactly. I need to talk to you."

"We can all sit down in the next room," Cade said.

She pointed at me. "I want to talk to *you*. Not him."

"Whatever you're here to say, it needs to be said in front of me, understand?" Cade said.

"You know what? I didn't want to come here," she said.

"Then why did you?" I asked.

"I dunno. I shouldn't have. This was a mistake. I'm outta here."

Cade stood in front of the door, blocking her from leaving. Veronica's eyes darted around like a jackrabbit, looking for an alternate way out.

I spread my hands out in front of me. "Can everyone dial down for a second?"

"I'm not the one causing problems," Veronica said. "*He* is."

"If you're only comfortable talking to me, that's fine," I said.

Cade glared at me. "It's not *fine*, Sloane. It's not your call. If she knows somethin', I need to know what it is."

I couldn't understand how he failed to see he was only making things worse. I assumed whatever she had to say was delicate in nature—something she didn't feel comfortable saying in front of him. I considered pulling him aside, but didn't. I couldn't leave our little flight risk alone.

"If it makes her more comfortable to talk to me, let her talk to me."

He shook his head.

Still blocked from leaving, Veronica seemed close to panicking. "I want to get outta here. Let me out. Coming here was a mistake."

"Please," I said. "Can you give us just a second to talk? Then if you still want to go, you can."

Cade's temper was nearing a breaking point. I joined him at the door, lowering my voice to a whisper. "Look, this girl's spooked, and you're not helping. Every second you refuse to budge decreases the chances of either of us finding out why she's really here."

"I don't like her tellin' me—"

I grabbed his arm, staring into his eyes. "Please. Let me handle this."

Upstairs, Maddie's bedroom door opened and shut, and Boo came bounding down the stairs. I scooped him up.

Cade flung his hands in the air and walked to our bedroom, slamming the door behind him. I glanced up. Maddie was at the top of the stairs, observing.

She yawned. "Go find a place to talk to this girl, and I'll deal with him. Leave it to me. He'll be okay."

I turned back to Veronica. "I'm sorry. He won't bother you anymore tonight. He's just on edge, you know? He's struggling to understand what happened to his daughter."

"I don't care. I can't talk to you around him. Not here."

I contemplated alternative options and shared them with Maddie. "Can I take her into the guesthouse?"

Maddie descended the stairs.

"You can, but I wouldn't. Police cordoned it off earlier today. I mean, I can still get you in there, but I'd talk somewhere else if I were you." She lifted her keys off a hook on the wall. "Take my car. Go for a drive. She'll get the privacy she needs, and I'll get some time to help Cade calm down."

I looked at Veronica, who nodded her agreement to the plan.

I handed Boo to Maddie, took the keys, grabbed my coat, and walked with Veronica to the car. Anxious to learn the reason for her late-night visit, I didn't go far, driving to a deserted strip mall parking lot not far from Maddie's house. I put the car in park, allowing it to idle, and waited for her to begin.

A minute passed and she hadn't said anything, and I didn't have the patience to wait. "Why are we here? What did you want to talk to me about?"

"Shelby said she told you about Paul Armstrong."

Bingo. We had a last name.

"He was her boyfriend, right?"

"I … guess you could call him that."

"Was he or wasn't he?"

She paused, then said, "He's married."

"Married? How old is this guy?"

"Thirty-three."

"*Thirty-three*? Was he aware he was dating a twenty-year-old college student?"

She nodded. "He knew."

It just kept getting better.

"I'm glad you came to me, but why not go to the police with this information instead?"

"I can't talk to the police. It's complicated."

"More complicated than Paul being married?" She was afraid. I got the impression it wasn't over what she'd just told me. There was something else. Something she hadn't said yet. "What is worrying you, Veronica? Maybe I can help."

"Shelby talked about you all the time. She idolized you, you know? She said she could trust you with anything."

If Shelby had really felt she could trust me, why did I feel like she'd hidden plenty?

"She thought it was cool that you and her dad were getting married," she said.

"We're not engaged. Not yet, anyway."

"Oh, Shelby told me you were getting married. She was really excited."

I felt the same sick, uneasy feeling I had in Maddie's lab. Cade had told Shelby of his plan to propose to me.

"Aside from the fact Shelby was dating a married man, is

there anything else you'd like to tell me? Because I get the feeling there is."

Veronica fidgeted with the zipper on her coat, sliding it up and down. "Shelby wanted to quit school because she'd already found a career where she'd make plenty of money."

"I don't understand. Shelby didn't have a job."

"Yes, she did. She was a professional escort."

CHAPTER 9

I sat there, stunned, not wanting to believe what Veronica had just said. She couldn't have been right. Not Shelby. There had to be some mistake, and yet Veronica had maintained a straight face when she'd said it. My instincts told me she was telling the truth. Shelby had always had a wild, carefree side, but sleeping with men for money? I didn't want it to make sense, but it did—the expensive handbag, the diamond earrings, the shoes she'd worn when I last saw her. If she really was an escort, I now knew for sure they weren't fakes or borrowed like Shelby had tried to get me to believe. They were the real deal.

"Are you telling me Shelby was a hooker?" I asked.

Veronica looked at me, laughed. "Uhh ... no. You're thinking of those chicks in the eighties who stood on street corners, waiting on some loser to pick them up so they could earn a bit of cash to support their drug habit. I get why you would think that though. It's because you're ..."

She stopped herself from saying the word she meant to say. *Old*. I was old. Old and behind the times apparently. "How does one become a professional escort at twenty? She's only been living on her own for a year and a half."

"Before she left for college, she met a girl in Wyoming who introduced her to the business. When she said she was moving to Salt Lake City, the girl said she had connections down here and she could hook Shelby up with a job where she could make all the money she wanted."

"What was the girl's name?"

"Heather Farnsworth, but her escort name was—"

"Sadie Steele."

The previous summer, Heather Farnsworth had been found dead inside of her pot dealer's home in Wyoming. She had been gunned down by a woman who'd discovered Heather was having extramarital relations with her husband.

"I worked Heather's murder case with Shelby's father, Cade. I even talked to Shelby about it. She never mentioned she knew Heather."

Veronica shrugged. "How could she?"

She was right. She couldn't. "How do you know all of this?"

"It doesn't matter."

"Sure it does. You worked with her, didn't you? You're an escort."

She stared outside at nothing. "It's not what you think."

I crossed my arms. "Enlighten me then. Explain it to me."

"Girls in the escort business are educated and smart. They come from good families. Famous families even sometimes."

"And the men? Do you expect me to believe they're decent guys too?"

"They are. Most are clean-cut professionals. Some own

their own companies, some run companies, and some are celebrities. Every one of them is thoroughly vetted before he's placed with a girl. They're not douchebags."

"And yet these guys hire call girls?"

"Shelby wasn't a hooker or a call girl. She was an escort, just like Heather."

"What's the difference?"

"Escorts are clean, classy, and trained. They look more like well-dressed supermodels. You've probably been around them before and didn't have a clue they were an escort and not the man's date. Escorts aren't just hired for sex. Sometimes a client needs a companion or a date, nothing more. Call girls charge less, and sex is part of the deal. And hookers ... well, everyone knows what they're like."

"Are you saying Shelby never had sex with the guys who hired her?"

Veronica opened the car door and stepped out.

"Where are you going?" I asked.

She glanced back at me. "Sorry. The last twenty-four hours have been rough. I'm a mess. I need to smoke. Care to join?"

"No, I'm fine."

I expected her to grab a pack of cigarettes out of her purse, but she didn't. She left her purse on the seat, closed the door, and pulled a slender pink vape pen out of her pocket. I'd heard of vaping before, but hadn't been exposed to it until now. Maybe I *was* getting old. I watched her suck the smoke through the vape and blow it into the air. While she was distracted, I took advantage of the moment by sticking my hand into her purse to see what I could find. I didn't get far before she turned back around, returning to the car for round two.

"Okay," she said. "Where were we?"

"I asked you if Shelby ever had sex with any of the men who hired her."

"Shelby's situation was unique."

Unique didn't answer the question.

"In what way?"

"The way it works at the company she worked for is that every girl goes out on practice dates while they're being trained. It familiarizes them with the process. No sex is involved. From there, they graduate to both sexual and non-sexual jobs. Shelby's first post-graduate job was with Paul."

"What happened?"

"He took her away for the weekend and became obsessed with her. When they returned, he told the agency he wanted Shelby all to himself. He offered to pay double the normal rate to have her date him exclusively."

"Did Shelby want to be with Paul too?"

"She felt something for him at first, I suppose; it just wasn't the same feeling Paul had for her. He showered her with gifts. That's why she kept seeing him. She thought she could make their arrangement seem exclusive to him while she still saw other men on the side."

"How did the agency react to Paul's offer?"

"They had spent time and money grooming her. He couldn't just make a demand and expect them to honor it. They talked to Shelby and agreed on a compromise."

"What was the compromise?"

"He'd pay double to see her for an entire year, and she had to keep accepting dates with other men—the arm-candy kind, not the sexual kind. It gave Shelby what she wanted, and made Paul feel like she didn't have a choice, even though she did."

I hugged my coat against my skin, the car's warmth doing little to keep an icy chill from coursing through me. The sudden discovery of Shelby's secret life was difficult for me to accept. What else didn't I know?

"Tell me more about Paul."

She shook her head. "I can't. I mean, I shouldn't. I've told you too much already."

"You have to, Veronica. Why else would you risk coming to me? You must suspect him of something or you wouldn't be here."

She slumped in her seat, kicking her feet up on the dash. "I don't think he's to blame for what happened. I like Paul. He's always been good to her. He found out what happened this morning, and he's devastated."

Maybe, or maybe he just wanted her to *think* he devastated in order to hide his crime of passion. "He could be putting on a show to cover up the fact he murdered her in a jealous rage."

"You don't know him. He loved her. He was trying to find a way to get rid of Elise, his wife, so he could keep seeing her."

"What do you mean *get rid* of her? Divorce?"

She shook her head. "He can't divorce her unless he's okay with being flat broke. The money he spent on Shelby was from his wife's inheritance, and they have a prenup. If the marriage dissolves, he leaves with nothing."

"Are you saying he planned to kill his wife?"

She shrugged. "I had a weird conversation with Shelby last month. She said she was worried Paul was going to do something to his wife. Apparently, Elise had found out Paul was seeing Shelby. Elise confronted him and said he needed to end it or she was cutting him off.

The words "do something" were open to interpretation. "Are you sure she meant he intended to kill her?"

"He told Shelby he had considered hiring a guy he knew to get rid of Elise, someone who could make her death look like an accident. Shelby thought he was joking until he said it was his only choice. He thought his wife was having him followed."

"Whoa. Wait a minute. I may not know everything Shelby was doing, but she was still a good kid, and she wouldn't have been on board with murder."

"She wasn't. She told him if anything happened to his wife, they were done."

"What did he say?"

"He hung up, and that was the last time he talked to her."

"Did Paul's wife know he hired escorts?"

She shrugged. "I dunno, but Shelby saw Elise right before she went home for Christmas."

"Where?"

"At a coffee shop."

"And Shelby was sure it was her?"

"She'd seen pictures of Elise before. Shelby went to the same coffee shop religiously every morning at the same time. The thing is—it's downtown, and Elise lives twenty-five minutes away, so it wasn't just a coincidence."

"Did they talk?"

She shook her head. "Elise gave Shelby a cold stare, and then watched Shelby from the time she got in line to the time she left. Shelby wasn't sure whether it was a scare tactic on

Elise's part, or if Elise just wanted to see the woman who had been seeing her husband. It really freaked Shelby out."

There it was, the real reason for Veronica's visit. She didn't blame Paul for Shelby's murder. She blamed his wife. "Is this why you're here? Do you think Elise had something to do with Shelby's murder?"

"I'm not sure. It's possible, I guess. There's one more possibility. Last month she started seeing someone new, a regular guy who had nothing to do with the escort business. She was crazy about him, and he had no idea she was an escort … well, not at first."

"What makes you suspect him?"

"One night he saw her leaving a hockey game. She was arm in arm with a couple of the players, and he lost it. She told him she knew the guys through one of her friends, but he didn't believe her. He seemed suspicious ever since, and then started questioning her about everything."

"Is his name Jesse?"

She raised a brow. "Yeah, how did you know?"

"She mentioned him to me when she was home. What else can you tell me about him?"

"His full name is Jesse Baldwin. He's twenty-four, and he works for Burns Construction."

"Do you have an address or a phone number?"

"I don't."

"What about Paul? Can you give me his information?"

She considered it. "I'll only give it to you if he never finds out it came from me. As far as I'm concerned, this conversation we're having never happened."

I nodded. "Deal."

I typed Paul's information into my phone for later, put the car in reverse, and headed back to Maddie's house. I parked, and we got out. Veronica walked toward her car, stopping halfway. "By the way, I guess there's something I should confess. My name's not really Veronica. I didn't want to come here tonight, but I knew I should. I'm the only one Shelby told about Paul's wife. The things I've said could get me in a lot of trouble. I have to protect myself."

I assumed she meant because she was an escort too.

"Why not contact the police, tell them what you told me? There are ways to give them information and remain anonymous."

She wiped a tear from her eye. "Like I said, I don't trust the police. Never have. But I cared about Shelby, and I knew I needed to tell someone. That's why I came to you."

CHAPTER 10

I leaned against the front door, the heaviness of the discussion I'd just had with "not Veronica" crushing down on me like I'd been trapped in an avalanche. I wanted to remain at the door, wanted to delay the inevitable conversation with Cade ... forever if possible. How could I tell him about his daughter? What could I possibly say to ease the pain of the blow I was about to deliver?

Nothing.

I could say nothing.

Except nothing wasn't an option.

"You've been gone over an hour. You okay?"

I opened my eyes and glanced around the corner. Cade sat on the sofa, his hands interlocked behind his head.

"No," I said. "I'm not all right."

"She gone?"

I nodded.

"What was she doing here? And how does she know Shelby?"

"I ... ahh ... she gave me some information I'm guessing the police don't know about yet."

"Like what?"

"She told me some alarming things about Shelby that are going to be hard for you to hear, but you need to hear it."

He patted the couch cushion with a hand. "You wanna come sit down and we can talk?"

I nodded and walked over, pausing a moment before sitting next to him. "You know what? Where's Maddie? She may as well hear this too."

Coffee gripped in each hand, Maddie entered the room as if on cue. She gave one to Cade and set the other on the table for herself. "Can I get you anything, Sloane?"

"Water."

"You got it."

Maddie returned with the water, handed it to me, and sat across from us.

"All right," Maddie said. "Let's hear it."

I went over everything I'd learned from "not Veronica." Watching Cade react to the news was like waiting for a teakettle to boil. The more I talked, the madder he became, until he launched off the couch in a tirade.

"Shelby would never stoop to bein' paid to entertain men. Y'ask me, this girl is the one guilty of somethin', and you just let her drive away without even knowin' her real name or how the hell we're supposed to find her again."

I swallowed the insult. "I lifted her driver's license out of her bag when she stepped outside for a smoke. Her name is Adele Winters."

"Yeah, well, Adele Winters is a liar. I don't believe a word she told you."

"Think about it, Cade. Why would she come here if she were guilty of something? She wouldn't have."

"Why are you takin' her side? You don't even know this girl."

I sighed. "This isn't about sides. It's about following every lead until we find the man responsible for Shelby's murder."

He flipped around, wagged a finger at Maddie. "I left my daughter in *your* care. I trusted you to tell me if there was somethin' goin' on with her. Sounds like she had nothin' but sketchy friends and sleazy boyfriends, and you were oblivious about all of it."

Maddie placed a hand on her hip. "Stop making assumptions, Cade. I only knew what she told me, and it sounds to me like she lied to all of us. I didn't know this Paul guy was married. Do you really think I would have been okay with it if I did?"

"Don't matter whether you did or didn't know. You let her down. You let us *all* down."

Maddie stretched her hand out in front of her. "Whoa. I get you're grieving, but get a freaking grip. You're way out of line. I allowed Shelby to stay in my guesthouse as a favor to you and Sloane since I'm so close to the university. I didn't sign up to micromanage her life, and I didn't sign up to be her babysitter. *You* were the parent. Not me. If you wanted to know what she was doing every minute of every day, you should have kept better tabs on her."

He shook his head. "I don't need this right now. I'm outta here."

He grabbed his boots and slipped them on.

I placed a hand on his shoulder. "Cade, where are you going? Hang on a—"

"What's the address?"

"Address?" I asked. "What address?"

"Paul's address. Give it to me."

I shook my head. "I know what you're thinking, and it isn't a good idea. You're angry. We don't know what is true and what isn't yet. You can't go after this guy this way."

He snatched my cell phone out of my hand and bolted for the door.

"Cade, don't," I said. "Leave it alone. Why don't you let me talk to Paul first? Or we can call Coop and tell him what happened. He'll look into it. He can get anyone to talk. I've seen him do it."

"You really think that asshole will do anything to help after the way he treated us in his office? I'm not takin' any chances. I'm handlin' this myself."

Before I could stop him, he'd found Maddie's keys, bolted out of the front door, and sped out of the driveway, leaving me standing on the porch, watching chunks of snow spraying from beneath the tires as he drove down the road.

"You know he's headed to Paul's house, right?" Maddie said, "and what he'll do once he gets there? He's not thinking straight."

I walked to the bedroom and checked the nightstand, even though I knew what I'd find. His gun was gone.

"He has my phone, Maddie. Can I borrow yours?"

She handed it over.

I made a call I didn't want to make, but we needed a vehicle, and we needed it now. "I'm sorry about the time, but I need your help. Can you come to Maddie's and pick us up? I'll explain everything when you get here."

CHAPTER 11

Hank's truck rolled to a stop in front of Maddie's house twenty minutes later, giving Cade a huge head start. I had tried calling him on Maddie's phone, even though I knew he wouldn't pick up ... and he didn't. I then debated whether or not to alert Coop about recent events. If I did, Cade would feel I had betrayed him. If I didn't and Cade pulled a gun on Paul, or worse, Coop would lock him up just for kicks. Under most circumstances, Cade was a rational man—the kind of guy who had always talked me down when I was about to make the wrong decision. All I could do now was pray he'd keep it together until we got there.

Maddie and I jumped into the back seat of Hank's truck.

Bonnie glanced back at us and frowned. "Sorry it took so long. We left the hotel right after you called, but between the snow on the road and the fog, it really slowed us down."

I hoped it had slowed Cade down too.

"I'm just glad you're here."

Hank backed out of the driveway. "Where are we headed, Sloane?"

"Draper. Get on the I-15 freeway, southbound."

"What's going on?" Bonnie asked. "Where's Cade? Why isn't he with you?"

I told her everything.

When I finished, she said, "It's heartbreaking to know my niece was involved in such a sleazy business, but I can't say I'm surprised. Since the moment she came out of her mother's womb, I knew she was going to be a firecracker, and she didn't disappoint. Even as a toddler, she always tested the limits."

"I'm worried about what Cade will do when he confronts Paul. He's not himself right now, Bonnie."

"If it turns out this man had something to do with what happened to Shelby, there's no telling what he'll do."

I glanced at Maddie who looked as worried as I was. I didn't call Coop, and I hoped it wasn't a mistake.

CHAPTER 12

Cade had parked Maddie's car haphazardly in Paul's driveway, leaving the driver's-side door wide open—not a good sign. Hank parked curbside, and everyone prepared to get out.

"I appreciate you two for driving me here, but I'd like to go in alone," I said.

Hank and Bonnie protested, and Maddie crossed her arms in front of her, sulking. It seemed everyone wanted in on the rescue mission.

"Look," I said, "all four of us barging into a house uninvited isn't a good idea. If I need backup, I'll let you know."

"He's lost control," Bonnie said. "Pulling him off the ledge isn't going to be easy. Not even for you."

I was well aware, but I remained firm in my decision. I exited the truck. As I neared the door, I heard Cade's booming voice echoing from inside the house.

"When I ask you a question, you answer it. Understand?!"

A man replied, "I ... can't. I ... can't ... breathe."

A woman shouted, "You're choking him!"

I sprinted inside, finding Cade in the living room. One of Cade's hands was wrapped around a man's throat. I assumed he was Paul. The other hand pressed the barrel of a gun against the man's temple.

A woman stood a few feet away. She was pint-sized, no more than five foot two, and tan. Italian, I guessed, with long, straight, dark hair and green, snakelike eyes. Beautiful. Far too beautiful to be married to the man in Cade's grip, a balding, plain-looking fellow with no remarkable features. Even if he *had* showered Shelby with gifts, I had no idea how she'd stomached him.

Although the woman looked alarmed, she did nothing to stop Cade from attacking the man, and I wondered why. Perhaps seeing Cade with a gun immobilized her, or perhaps she secretly relished the moment, knowing he'd cheated and glad he was getting what he deserved.

"Cade, take your hands off of him," I said.

He glanced back at me, irritated. "You shouldn't be here, Sloane."

"Neither should you. There's a better way to handle this."

"Don't need your advice."

"I called the police," the woman said. "They're on their way."

I turned toward her. "Are you Elise?"

She nodded.

"And he's Paul?"

She nodded again.

I placed a hand on Cade's shoulder. "Come on. Let's go."

Cade shook his head. "No way. Not until this piece of shit tells me everything I want to know about my daughter."

"Look at him!" I said. "There's barely any color left in his face. When Coop finds you here, he'll charge you with assault, breaking and entering, and anything else he can throw at you."

Seconds ticked by. I waited, not knowing if anything I'd said had resonated. Having just lost Shelby, he seemed numb, devoid of feeling, like nothing fazed him and nothing could get through.

"Please, Cade. Don't do this."

"Listen to her," Elise said. "She's right."

"Stay out of it," Cade said.

"I have been," she said. "Look, I understand. My husband is a dirt bag. He deserves what's happening, but he's not worth going to jail for."

It wasn't my words, but Elise's that made the difference. Cade loosened his grip on Paul and took a few steps back, his fingers still gripping the gun. Paul slid to the floor, coughing and gagging like he'd been freed from a hangman's noose.

I held out my hand. "Give me the gun, Cade."

He shook his head and slid it into the holster strapped to his hip.

I turned toward Elise. "Can we talk for a minute?"

"Talk? After what just happened? You're kidding, right?"

"Do you know who we are and why we're here?"

"Of course I do." She tipped her head toward Cade. "He's Shelby's father, and you must be her mother. I don't care."

"I'm a private investigator. Shelby was like a daughter to me."

She shrugged. "So, what … I'm supposed to feel bad for you now? You broke into our home without permission."

"I didn't *break in*," Cade said. "The door wasn't locked. I said I was comin' inside when I entered."

"Yeah," she laughed, "*after* you had already done it."

"He's just looking for answers," I said. "We both are."

"I'm not interested in excuses. I know why you're here."

I surveyed the room. It was meticulous and rich, with everything in its place. I felt the absence of children, and yet, there was an eight-by-ten portrait of a young woman on the wall. I considered appealing to her nurturing side, if she had one. "Have you ever lost a child?"

She laughed. "Of course not. We don't have children. We have cats. Two of them."

I pointed to the portrait. "This girl looks like she's close to Shelby's age. Who is she?"

"My niece. And she is. She's eighteen."

"If your sister lost her unexpectedly, imagine how she'd feel, imagine what she'd do to get justice for her."

Voice garbled and strained, Paul muttered, "Get out. Get out of my house."

"Shut your mouth," Elise snapped at him. "This isn't *your* house. It's mine, paid for with *my* money."

"Elise, back me up," he pleaded. "You saw what he did to me. You saw it all. He almost killed me."

Cade's eyes narrowed at Paul, like he was prepared to finish the job if the man didn't shut it.

"Stop blaming everyone else for your problems," Elise said. "*You* did this. You brought this on, and now they're here because of it."

"Like I said before, we're just trying to find out what happened to Shelby," I said.

"We don't know anything about her murder," Elise said, "or why anyone would harm her. It's the truth. I wouldn't lie to you, not about something like that."

I didn't know why, but I believed her. "Your husband had been seeing Shelby off and on for a long time. You found out recently and showed up at the coffee shop she frequented."

Paul looked like he'd been blindsided. "What is she talking about? You followed Shelby? When?"

Elise flashed him an icy glare. "I told you to keep quiet."

She pivoted, walked to the sofa, and sat down, sitting straight up with both hands over her knees like she was waiting on the help to bring out a fresh pot of tea. "I wasn't aware of Paul's relationship with Shelby until recently."

"When did you find out?"

"A couple of weeks ago. I was getting into my car and noticed what looked like a flyer sticking out from beneath one of my windshield wipers. I grabbed it, turned it over, and realized I was wrong. It wasn't a flyer. It was a photo of Shelby and Paul. They were kissing."

Cade clenched his jaw, but kept quiet.

"Do you have any idea who left it on your car, or why?" I asked.

She shrugged. "Obviously someone who wanted me to know Paul was having an affair."

"Is that all there was? Just a photo?"

She stood. "Actually, no. There's more."

She rose and crossed the room, walking to a desk in the corner. She pulled the top drawer open, riffling around until she found what she was looking for—a folded piece of paper. I glanced at a clock hanging on the wall. Fifteen minutes had passed since I'd arrived, and the police weren't there, even though she'd said she called them.

Curious.

Equally as curious was her sudden shift in demeanor. She'd gone from withholding information to being overly generous. I wondered why. She didn't strike me as a compassionate person, making me wonder if her sudden willingness to talk had more to do with humiliating Paul in front of an audience and reminding him she had the upper hand.

Elise unfolded the sheet of paper and handed it to me. She was right. The girl was Shelby. She was standing with Paul outside of a coffee shop, kissing. On the back of the paper, written in black ink it said: *Ask your husband about his extramarital affair with Shelby. And watch your back. Your husband can't be trusted. You're in danger.*

"It looks like someone printed this off of a computer," I said. "How did you know the girl in this photo was Shelby?"

"I didn't at first. I went online and took a look at the call history. There were numerous calls to the same Wyoming area code. I plugged the number into Google and found her name. I assumed she was the one who left the photo on my car."

"How did you find her?"

"Once I had a name, I found her profile on Facebook. She'd taken several selfies at the same coffee shop. I went there three times before I finally saw her there. I wanted to confront her, but somehow seeing her in person made me change my mind."

"Why?" I asked.

"She was just a kid, and I realized whether or not she knew he was married, it wasn't her I was mad at—it was my husband. She didn't know me. It wasn't personal, and it wasn't the first time he'd cheated, or the first time he'd hired an escort."

Paul pushed himself off the floor and stood, looking shocked to hear Elise was well informed about his private life.

"It was an innocent kiss, Elise. We weren't sleeping together. I'd never do anything to hurt you. You know that."

He took a step toward her. Cade blocked him with his arm.

"Stay where you are," Elise warned. "Don't come anywhere near me, Paul."

"Why didn't you tell me about the photo?" Paul asked. "We could have talked about it and cleared things up."

"I wasn't interested in a confrontation where you'd do the same thing you always do when this happens—lie to my face and then grovel until I take you back. You don't love me anymore. You love my money, and the well has run dry."

A stunned Paul said, "I don't follow."

"Don't you?"

They locked eyes, and she grinned, savoring the moment. She crossed one leg over the other and reclined back on the sofa. "I suppose now is as good a time as any to let you know it's over between us. Evidence of your affair has been given to my lawyer."

"Let's talk about this, honey," Paul said. "It's not what you think. So we talked on the phone a bunch of times. Big deal. It meant nothing—not to me. She probably left the photo on the car to cause problems between us. She wanted a relationship, and I wouldn't give her one. I was flattered, of course, but I told her it wasn't possible. I loved my wife."

Elise tossed her head back and laughed. "She's dead, Paul. She's not here to defend herself. And you're a liar. Save your breath for your lawyer."

"Oh, come on, Elise. You're just angry. I don't need a lawyer."

"You will. I've retained Katerina Smirnoff."

"Katerina who?"

"The lawyer everyone refers to as The Barracuda."

Paul dropped to his knees, reaching for Elise. "Please, Elise. Don't do this. I'll do anything to make it up to you. Anything you want."

Elise glanced at Cade and then me. "We have some talking to do that isn't your business. It's time for you two to go."

"I'm not finished," Cade said. "I still have questions."

"We're not responsible for what happened to your daughter," Elise said. "Deep down I believe you know that. Paul was here with me at the time she died. I have no reason to be dishonest. If I could put him in prison, believe me, I would, but he's not the guy you're after."

Paul's eyes flooded with tears, although I believed it had more to do with the money he stood to lose than any sentiment he felt for Elise or Shelby. "You can't do this. You can't divorce me. I'm begging you, honey. Please."

"I can," Elise said "And don't you worry, I'll make sure you leave this marriage with everything you had when you came into it—absolutely nothing."

Cade joined me at the door.

His life in ruins, Paul remained on his knees, his head buried in his hands.

Elise walked us out.

"I feel there's something I should tell you before I leave," I said.

She raised a brow. "What is it?"

"I believe whoever left you the note was telling the truth about you being in danger."

"How so?"

"Last night, one of Shelby's friends said Paul was willing to have you killed so he could be with Shelby without losing your money. I have no idea how credible this friend is, but I thought you should know."

Elise swished a hand through the air. "You see him in there, groveling on the floor like an infant? He's weak. He's no killer."

"Just be careful," Cade said. "I've seen my share of men like him before. Don't underestimate what he's capable of, ma'am."

She reeled back. "Thanks for your concern, but I'm capable of handling myself. I'd like to know the name of Shelby's friend. My lawyer will want to talk to her."

"We don't know her name," I said.

"What do you mean?"

"I'd rather not go into details right now. Allow me some time to find her again, and I'll see what I can arrange."

"Fair enough." She turned, winking at Cade. "In the spirit of sharing, I never called the police. When you attacked Paul, I'd considered it, but for my own selfish reasons, I suppose I wanted to see him get roughed up. I figured he wasn't in real danger. You pointed your gun, but you never cocked it."

Cade frowned. "I ... uhh ... I shouldn't have ... I didn't mean to scare you. I shouldn't have entered your house like I did. It's not who I am, believe me."

"Mr. McCoy, it's all right. There's no need to say anything more."

She turned and walked back to the house. Cade slid his hand inside mine and gave it a squeeze. He opened the truck door, and I started to climb in, but halted when a bloodcurdling scream reverberated behind me.

A woman's scream.

Elise.

We made it halfway back before we heard gunshots coming from inside the house.

One pop.

Then two.

Cade jerked his gun out of the holster, barreling through the front door.

"Elise!" I yelled. "Are you okay? Where are you?"

There was no reply, just a frightening quiet.

We sprinted through room after room, searching, finding nothing and no one. Then we heard Paul lashing out, his voice crazy, from somewhere upstairs. He sounded enraged and hysterical, a different man than the one I'd witnessed moments before.

"You're not going to take everything from me!" Paul said. "Oh no. Not going to take it from me now, are ya? Say it!"

"I'm not ... I'm not going to take it, Paul," Elise said. "I'm sorry. I was angry. I didn't mean it. Please, put the gun down."

Cade ascended the stairs. I followed, the sound of Elise's desperate cries penetrating through the other side of a closed door.

"That's right, you bitch," Paul said. "That's right! You think you'll have the last laugh now? Huh? Do ya?"

Elise was sobbing. "Stop it, Paul! Stop it!"

Cade twisted the knob on the door. It was locked. Gunfire rang out again. Cade hammered his boot into the door, and it broke open. Inside the room was Elise, face down in a pool of blood, and Paul sitting in front of her, waving the gun above his head, laughing.

CHAPTER 13

I dialed 9-1-1 and gave Paul's address to the operator. She repeated it back to me and gave me the usual spiel about remaining on the line, but I didn't. I hung up. I had another, much more worrisome, call to make.

Coop answered with, "You better have a good reason for calling this early. What is it?"

"I'm at 3742 Arrowhead Lane in Draper."

"Yeah, and? Am I supposed to know whose house that is?"

"Paul and Elise Armstrong. He just killed his wife. You should probably get over here."

He sighed. "Why are *you* there?"

"Paul knew Shelby McCoy. The easiest way to explain it would be to say they were having an affair, but it's a little more complicated."

"And you know this how?"

"It's too much to tell you over the phone. I'll fill you in on all the details when you get here."

"No, you'll fill me in now," he grunted.

For the second time in five minutes, I abruptly ended a call. Coop called back, and I didn't answer, a decision I knew I'd pay for later. He had a habit of keeping a running tally of everything I'd ever done wrong. Hanging up on him added a significant number of points to his Sloane Shit List. In another hour I imagined the amount would soar even higher. Much, much higher.

I sent Bonnie and Hank away, leaving Maddie, Cade, and me to deal with Coop when he arrived. We discussed our stories, knowing the importance of them all matching up. Aside from Elise's dead body, we had an additional problem. Paul had finger-shaped bruises on the right side of his neck—bruises too large to be made by anyone else's hand but Cade's. They wouldn't go unnoticed.

Cade had stuck Paul in a kitchen chair, securing his wrists with some duct tape he found in a drawer. Paul had been spouting gibberish since the last gunshot, most of it too hard to understand. It was like murdering his wife had flipped a switch in his brain, and he'd had a psychotic break. I wasn't so sure though. He seemed to be faking, his outburst nothing more than the act of a man planning to plead insanity.

Coop arrived before the paramedics, accompanied by two police officers he called Fassbender and Sheraton. He walked into the kitchen, slid a chair out from the table, and sat in front of Paul. "You kill your wife?"

"I have a wife. Her name is Elise."

"Correction. You *had* a wife. She's dead. You shot her this morning. Remember?"

"I wouldn't kill my wife. I love her." He glanced upstairs.

"Elise, can you come down here? We have visitors."

I had to fist my hands to keep myself from clapping at his impeccable acting skills.

Coop's nostrils flared along with his lack of patience. "So you're telling me you don't remember pointing a gun at your wife's head and pulling the trigger?"

"I … no."

Coop leaned forward. "You shot your wife, Paul. She's dead."

Paul shook his head repeatedly. "No. No. No. She'll be coming downstairs in a minute. You'll see."

"You're right. She *will* be coming downstairs, only it will be inside of a body bag."

Paul sat still for a time and then he enacted phase two: waterworks. "Why are you saying this to me? Why are you telling me I murdered my wife? How could you be so cruel?"

Coop leaned back in the chair, crossing his arms. "All right. You want to stick to your story, fine. We'll save it for later and change topics. Did you know Shelby McCoy?"

"Shelby? Yeah, she's a nice girl."

"She's dead too."

Paul attempted to rock back and forth, but the hand restraints only allowed for limited mobility. "Oh, yes. I remember now. I saw it on the news today."

"Did you have anything to do with Shelby McCoy's death?"

Paul's eyes shifted from Coop to Cade, and for a split second, he grinned before craning his neck, exposing the finger marks. "My neck hurts."

Asshole.

He *was* faking it.

Coop leaned in, pulling down the collar of Paul's pajama

shirt. He inspected the bruises and then jerked his head toward Cade. Cade offered no explanation, which was explanation enough for Coop, who scooted the chair back and stood.

"Fassbender, I'm tagging out," Coop said. "See if you can get this idiot to stop talking nonsense. Sheraton, take McCoy into the living room and get his story. Be sure to ask about the bruises. Maddie and Sloane, you're with me. Where's the woman?"

Maddie pointed upstairs.

"Well, let's have a look at her," he said.

We followed Coop to the bedroom. He crouched down in front of Elise, inspecting the bullet hole in her forehead. "She died right away, then?"

"She did," I said.

He stood back up, canvassing the room, his eyes coming to rest on the gun. "That where he was standing when he shot her?"

"Yes," I said. "We've been careful not to move or touch anything since it happened."

"Sloane, why is it every time you're involved in any case of mine, someone winds up getting killed? You're like a death magnet."

"I had nothing to do with Paul's decision to murder his wife."

"You were here when it happened. You had *something* to do with it."

"We were outside the first time he fired the gun."

He raised a brow. "Outside doing what?"

"Leaving."

He slid a hand down his face. "Give me the details, start to finish. And *don't* leave anything out."

I told him about the girl who came to the house, and how Cade had reacted upon learning about his daughter's line of work, and of Shelby and Paul's relationship.

"Cade only came here to talk," I said. "He just wanted answers."

"Answers, huh? That why the guy's neck looks like it's been branded?"

I shrugged. "So the guy has a sensitive neck. He'll live."

"Tell me about Paul shooting his wife. Why did he do it?"

"Cade confronted Paul about his affair with Shelby. Turns out his wife already knew about it. She chose this morning to tell him she had filed for divorce. Since they had a prenup, if they divorced, he left the marriage with nothing. He begged her to call off the divorce, and she refused."

"And then?"

"She asked us to leave. We were on our way out, heard two shots, and ran back into the house. They were here, in this room, with the door locked. She was still alive. He was trying to get her to say she wouldn't go through with the divorce. When she finally agreed, he shot her anyway. Cade kicked the door in, but it was too late. She was already dead."

Fassbender poked his head into the room. "Chief, I need a minute."

Coop left the room, and the paramedics arrived. Downstairs I heard Coop and Cade talking downstairs.

"This is stupid," Cade said. "You know it is."

"I warned you," Coop replied. "I told you to stay away from the investigation, to let my guys do the police work. If you wouldn't have barged in here like some hothead and assaulted the guy, maybe the woman would still be alive."

"I had nothin' to do with what happened to her."

"Save it," Coop said. "I don't care."

I headed downstairs and watched Paul being escorted out the front door. Cade was in the kitchen, his wrists zip-tied behind his back like he was a criminal.

"What the hell are you doing, Coop?" I asked.

"You want to join him? Keep talking."

Fine. I will.

"You don't need to do this," I said.

Coop squinted. "You should have asked me for help instead of allowing him to go off halfcocked this morning." He looked at Fassbender. "Take him to the station."

"And do what with him?" Fassbender asked.

Coop made eye contact with me and said, "I haven't decided yet. Just take him there."

He hadn't decided? It wasn't like Coop to offer leniency. What was he up to, and why?

"Come on, Coop," I said. "You're being ridiculous."

"It's all right, Sloane," Cade said. "I'll go. Everything will be fine."

Fassbender walked Cade out the front door, and Coop turned his attention on me. "You two girls get out of here. And Sloane, the same thing I said to Cade goes for you too. Back off this case. This is your last warning."

It had been a rough couple of days. I hadn't slept. Whatever filter I had on occasion no longer existed, and I wasn't leaving without getting my digs in. "Don't threaten me. I still have a license to practice here. That girl last night—she didn't come to *you*, she came to *me*."

"And look at the disaster it turned out to be."

Before I had the chance to make matters worse, Maddie leaned in and whispered, "Come on, let's go. None of this will help you find out what happened to Shelby."

For once, I listened.

CHAPTER 14

I was about to retain The Barracuda's services on Cade's behalf when I found out it was no longer necessary. Coop had released Cade on one condition—Cade had to return to Wyoming until the investigation was over. If he refused, he would be charged with breaking and entering and aggravated assault, two items a chief of police didn't need on public record.

Hank picked up Cade, and I met with Bonnie, who had asked for some alone time with me before they all returned to Wyoming.

I found Bonnie hunched over the fireplace in the lobby of the hotel where she'd been staying, nibbling on a chocolate chip cookie. I stripped my coat off, folded it over a leather chair, and joined her. "You wanted to see me?"

She smiled, the wrinkles on her face seeming more prominent today than before. "It's a good thing we're going back. Cade will need my help with the funeral arrangements, and besides, it feels like we're all in the way down here."

"I'm worried about him, Bonnie. I need to stay, but I feel like I'm abandoning him. Without me around to help him through all of this—"

She squeezed my shoulder. "We'll make sure he's not alone. He has us, and he understands. You should remain here. Knowing you're going to continue looking for answers will make it easier for him to leave."

In a way, I agreed. In another, I didn't. He'd worry, not just about whether or not the police would find Shelby's killer, but also about the risks of me going after the killer.

"We want you to stay until Shelby's murder is solved," she said. "I watched you work the Tate case, and then I watched you get baby Finn back for Jack. The way you figure things out, the way you solve things, it's unique. You're not like everyone else, Sloane. You're different. And right now I believe different is what we need."

Different.

I supposed I was, except it wasn't the kind of different that made me feel cool or special. I'd always felt like more of an outcast, the woman who stood in a room full of people, listening to a keynote address everyone understood but me. I saw above the speaker's message, beyond it. Where others found understanding, I found holes and gaps. Questions, so many questions, swirling, and festering, and solving—my mind an endless wanderer that never shut off.

"I'll keep you informed on what I find out and drive back for the funeral," I said.

She turned away from the fire and stuck a hand inside her purse, pulling out an envelope. She handed it to me. "This is for you."

I stood there, staring at it, knowing what it was and why she was giving it to me. "No, Bonnie, I can't. Keep it."

"You can. Go on. I'm hiring you to solve Shelby's murder. I have just as much right to hire you as anyone else."

I pushed the envelope away, rejecting it. "No, Bonnie. I don't want it. Shelby was my family too. I don't want the money."

She slid it into my hand, and I dropped it back into her purse like it was a hot potato. She grimaced, pulled it back out, folded it, and stuffed it into the pocket of my coat.

"Take it whether you want to or not. Cade's unable to help you, and even if he was, he doesn't have the ability to think clearly. And this Coop fellow has my insides all knotted up. The thought of that man heading up the search for Shelby's killer doesn't sit well with me. The man's a horse's ass from what I hear."

It was a fitting, accurate description, but not entirely fair.

"I know how Coop comes across, but there's a lot more to him than what anyone sees. I've known him for a long time. He saved my life once, and he's saved the lives of people I care about. No matter how crass he seems, no one will try harder to find Shelby's killer than he will."

Except me.

Hank pulled the truck around the front of the hotel, shifting into park while Cade got out and headed inside.

Bonnie pulled me in for a hug. "I feel better leaving knowing you're looking out for our family's interests."

"I'll do everything I can."

She smiled and walked through the revolving door, patting Cade on her way out. He approached me, pressing his lips against mine.

"Are you okay?" I asked.

He shrugged. "I dunno. Not really. I feel bad about all this, about leavin' you."

"You're not leaving me. You don't have a choice."

"It doesn't feel right though. Seems like I should be takin' you back with me."

"I have to stay. I have to find the man who killed Shelby."

"No, you don't."

"I'll be all right. Try not to worry."

He stepped back, resting his hands on my shoulders. "I'll always worry. Be careful. Don't do anything crazy. Promise me. I can't lose you too."

"I'll be fine, Cade. I promise."

CHAPTER 15

The man stood across from Bonnie and Hank's hotel, watching everyone say goodbye. From the looks of things, Cade appeared to be returning to Wyoming, and Sloane would stay behind.

Good.

It would be much easier for him to divide and conquer this way.

He took one last drag on his cigarette and flicked it to the ground, stubbing it out with the bottom of his shoe. He thought about leaving, but he couldn't tear his eyes away from Cade and Sloane, holding hands, standing together beside the truck for one last embrace. The embrace was long. Too long. It made the man uncomfortable.

Get on with it already.

Leave.

Viewing such tenderness between two people turned his stomach, like a virus had entered his body and quickly spread.

Anger.

Slow, festering anger.

His heart beating faster and faster.

He reached out, clutching a tree for support, inhaling and then exhaling and then inhaling again.

Focus.

Remember what you're here for and why.

You're in control.

It's all going according to plan.

Cade gripped the handle of the door, but then leaned back to Sloane, whispering something in her ear. For a moment it looked like she might cry, but she didn't.

Seeing the display of emotion between them was almost like witnessing two lovers on a movie screen, a magical connection that seemed too unrealistic to be real. For a fleeting moment the man was reminded of a time in his own life when he too had been in love. A time so long ago, he strained to remember it.

Over the years he'd been with plenty of women. A few of them he'd even cared for on a marginal, detached level. The rest served a single purpose—a warm body on a cold, lonely night. He had only ever felt real love for a woman once, and that woman had been his wife, and when he lost her, he lost everything.

CHAPTER 16

A flashy red mustang was parked in the driveway when I returned to Maddie's. I found her in the kitchen, leaning over a newspaper, her hair pinned up in two buns on the side of her head like she was a blond Princess Leia.

"Hey," she said. "Come here. I need to talk to you."

"You're not working today?"

Maddie folded the newspaper in half and tossed it into the trash. "I took some time off to help you, if you'll let me. After everything that's happened, I feel like I need to do something, especially since Cade seems irritated with me."

"He didn't mean what he said last night."

"Oh, I know."

I walked over to the trashcan and looked inside, seeing a piece of a headline above a photo of Shelby's face. It read: *Innocence Lost. The Secret Life of a Female Escort.* I reached down and fished the paper out.

Maddie placed a hand on my wrist. "Don't read it. Not now. It can wait."

"It's okay. I want to know what they said."

I wriggled my hand free of her grasp and unfolded the paper. The press had discovered Shelby's secret life, although it was unclear how. The article loosely attributed her death to the business she was in, even though it was obviously speculation. There was no actual proof.

"It could be worse," Maddie said. "They don't know the name of the agency, how long she worked there, or how many men were involved."

"Who do you think talked? Paul? There's no way Coop leaked it. He despises the press just as much as I do."

She shrugged. "Who knows? My guess is someone was paid for information, maybe a coworker of Shelby's."

"Whose car is parked outside?"

"Umm … it's … ahh … well, that's what I was trying to talk to you about when you walked in here. You've been so busy, and he was on vacation, and now he's back, and—"

"Now *who's* back?"

"You know how Coop told you his detective was out of town? Well, he's in the living room, waiting to talk to you."

I stared at her for a moment, wondering why she was being so cryptic.

"You're making me nervous," I whispered. "Do I know him?"

She nodded.

No matter how bad he was, he wouldn't top Coop.

"Just tell me who it is."

I heard footsteps, someone walking toward the kitchen. Whoever the mystery man was, I was about to find out.

"Been a while, Sloane," he said.

I didn't even need to turn. I recognized the voice. Leaning

against a wall by the kitchen's entrance was Nick Calhoun, a former Park City detective and my former boyfriend.

"Nick. What are you doing here?"

"Coop called me and said there was a case he needed help on."

"No, I mean, why are *you* here? Why would Coop call you about the case?"

"I work for him now."

He worked for him?

I'd remembered Coop saying his detective would speak to me once he returned to town, but I would have never believed that person was Nick. In the past, they had always butted heads. I wondered what had changed.

"*You're* his new detective? I didn't think you two liked each other, at least you didn't when I lived here."

"We don't always get along now either."

"Then why did he choose you?"

"Coop's an unconventional guy. He's more interested in how good I am at what I do than what he thinks of me personally. I hear the victim on the case is your boyfriend's daughter. Guess you broke things off with the suit?"

The "suit" he was referring to was another former boyfriend, Giovanni Luciana.

"A few years ago, yes."

"And you ... live in Wyoming? Really?"

"For now. Why?"

"Huh. Never figured you'd end up there."

Coop was familiar with my history with Nick, making me wonder if he sent him over to "handle me," make sure I stayed out of the way.

"Just to be clear, I'm here until I find out what happened

to Shelby," I said. "Coop won't stop me from investigating her murder, and neither will you."

"I didn't come here to stop you. Coop brought me up to speed about an hour ago, and I was hoping we could help each other out."

"Why would *you* want to help *me*? In the past, you had a hard time with me being a private investigator."

"It's different now."

"In what way?"

"For one, we're not in a relationship anymore."

I slipped onto one of the barstools at the counter, clasped my hands together. "You're right. We're not. And if you're thinking this is some way for you to get back with me, it isn't?"

"Sloane, listen. You don't need to—"

"I mean it, Nick. Even if I were single, it wouldn't change anything between us. We weren't good for each other, and I don't need you here now micromanaging my every move."

"Are you finished? Can I talk?"

I shrugged. "If you must."

He shook his head. "You know what? Forget it. I thought we could move past this and talk through the case like adults, but I don't think we can. For whatever reason, you still have a chip on your shoulder."

He spun around.

"I see you're still the same arrogant, pushy man I knew before," I said.

Walking away, he said, "And you're still hard-headed and stubborn. I'm married, by the way. Happily. Going on a year now, so whatever notion you had in your head about what I'm really doing here, you're wrong."

CHAPTER 17

The following morning, I found Maddie meditating on a large, square ottoman in the center of her room. "When you're finished, I'd like to see the crime scene and Shelby's room."

She opened her eyes, frowned. "You interrupted me, and it's not like I can get back to my peaceful place now. I'm finished."

I should have apologized, but I didn't.

"I just want to get going today. I also need to find this Jesse Baldwin kid, and see what he has to say."

"So we're ignoring what happened with Nick last night?" Maddie asked. "You went to bed after he left and refused to talk to me about it. Now you need something, and suddenly everything is okay?"

"You should have told me Nick worked for Coop, and that he was married. I feel like an idiot."

"I have no control over the things you say. It's not my fault."

"I wouldn't have said what I did if I'd known."

"I didn't slight you on purpose. I've been preoccupied since Shelby died. We all have. And the last time I offered to give you an update on Nick's life, you said you didn't ever want to know anything about him again. I was trying to think of a subtle way to tell you. I just hadn't come up with it yet. Kind of low priority, everything considered."

Maddie lifted her chin, defiant.

I leaned against the wall. "I'm sorry. I didn't mean to snap at you. It's been a long few days. I feel like I'm losing it."

She shrugged. "I get it. We're all struggling."

Everything was so heavy. We needed a change, something to lighten the mood, even if only for a moment.

"You want to hear something crazy?"

She smiled. "Always."

"The other day when we found out about Shelby, you couldn't get ahold of me because I was in the mountains with Cade. He was proposing."

Her eyes widened. "Oh, geez. Talk about bad timing. What did you say?"

"I didn't get the chance to say anything. He asked, and before I could respond, Bonnie and Hank drove up."

"So, tell me about the proposal. What did he do? How did he ask?"

I told her.

She raised a brow. "Did you have any idea he was going to pop the question before he did it?"

"I was putting some shirts away in his dresser drawer a few weeks ago and saw the box. I wasn't sure when he planned to ask, but it was obvious what kind of box it was, and it hadn't been there long."

"I knew it! You're the absolute worst when it comes to surprises."

And yet my life had been filled with too many of them, and not often the good kind.

"At least I didn't open the box," I said. "Do you have any idea how much restraint it took to know it was there and not do anything about it?"

"It gave you time to think about your answer though. Do you *want* to marry him?"

It was a hard question to answer.

It depended on the day.

"I like the way things are now, but I can see us married. We're good together. He gets me, and most men don't. I have imagined our wedding, but Shelby was always there with us. It feels so different now, like it wouldn't be the same without her. And he's suffering. It will be some time before he recovers."

"He *will* recover though."

Yes, but he'd never be the same.

"For now the proposal is on hold." I held out a hand, helping Maddie to her feet. "Let's check out the guesthouse."

"If Coop finds out we're over there, he'll—"

"It's not like we're trespassing. It's *your* guesthouse on *your* property. And since when have you cared about what Coop thinks?"

"It's different this time. It's Shelby. I don't want him to do to you what he did to Cade. I can't help but feel he's watching your every move."

I assumed as much, which was why he'd sent Nick, his mini minion.

"If I'm going to find answers, I have to poke around the

same way I would if I was working any other case. I can't worry about how it will affect Coop."

Or how it would affect me.

She unwrapped a stick of gum and popped it into her mouth. "You're right. I'm in."

A few minutes later, we walked through Maddie's back yard, ducking beneath strips of police tape on the guesthouse porch like we were going for a gold medal in a limbo contest. Maddie inserted her key into the door, and I followed her inside. We stood in silence at first, taking it all in, the heaviness of the loss leaving me gutted. Pain and suffering were familiar, parts of my life that had made me tough, but sometimes I didn't want to be tough anymore.

"They took a lot of her personal things into evidence," Maddie said. "Not sure what you're looking for or what's left to find."

"There's only one thing I'm interested in."

I glanced at a small, white, wooden table. I didn't see what I was looking for, which alarmed me. "I gave Shelby a plant several months ago when I visited. A succulent. She used to keep it on the center of the table, and now it's gone. Police wouldn't care about a plant, right? I suppose they could have moved it. Any idea where it is?"

"Shelby bought a few floating shelves for her bedroom wall recently, and it seems like I saw a plant or two there."

Maddie was right. I found the succulent resting on the middle shelf of her bedroom wall. I lifted it up, handed the base piece to Maddie, and returned the plant to the shelf.

"What are you doing?" she asked. "Why give me this?"

I reached out my hand, and she handed the base back to me. "You'll see."

The six-inch-square base consisted of two pieces, a top and bottom that sealed shut when twisted, making it look like one single piece. I unscrewed it, pulling the two segments apart.

Maddie stared in disbelief. "You're kidding me. I don't believe it."

"I gave this to her when she moved, to keep her money in or anything she wanted to hide or keep private."

"She was living with me though, not a college dorm. She didn't need to worry about anyone stealing her stuff."

The tone of Maddie's voice made me feel like I'd offended her.

"It had nothing to do with you, Maddie. I knew she would have friends over, and if she left the wrong things sitting around, they might have been too enticing not to take."

"Well, are you going to show me what's in there, or what?"

I lifted the lid, set it on the bed, and held the base in my hand. Maddie reached in, grabbing a money clip fastened over a stack of folded hundred-dollar bills. She counted it out. Two thousand dollars. "Wow. That's a nice chunk of cash for a girl her age."

"I wouldn't be surprised if there's more money stashed somewhere else too."

Maddie clipped the money back together, set it to the side, and reached for a stack of black business cards. The cards were simple, and contained only two pieces of information—Shelby's first name and a phone number.

I looked at the number. "It's not her number."

"Let's call it and see what happens."

"No, don't. Not yet."

"Why not? I can lower my voice enough to pass as a guy."

She proceeded to give me a less-than-impressive demonstration of a male voice, and I nixed the idea again.

She dropped the cards back into the box and frowned. "I hate this! I hate knowing I was clueless about what she was doing with her life. I should have spent more time with her. Cade was right, ya know? You two left her in my care, and I was off doing my own thing all the time. I should have paid more attention."

"She was old enough to make her own decisions, and she did. We were all in the dark. Shelby chose this life. I keep asking myself why, but I'll probably never know the answer. She had a loving family, a father who was always there for her, and a good life. It's not like she needed attention from these guys, and she wasn't broke either. Cade provided her with more than enough money to live on while she was here."

"I don't think it has anything to do with Cade," Maddie said. "But what about Wendy? She wasn't the best mother. Actually, she wasn't a mother at all. Do you think Shelby felt abandoned?"

I shook my head. "I don't know. The last time Shelby saw Wendy was a couple years ago. It was rocky at first, but they parted on okay terms, probably better terms than they had ever been on before."

I grabbed the last item in the plant base, a folded piece of paper with a photo printed on it.

"Hey," Maddie said. "Is this the same photo you told me about, the one Elise showed you at her house?"

"Yeah, it is."

It seemed Shelby was the one who had left the photo on Elise's car after all. I flipped it over, inspecting the words written on the back. The verbiage was similar, but a few of the words had been scratched out.

"It looks like she printed this one, wrote on it, and then didn't like what she said and decided to print out another one and change the wording," I said.

"Why would she keep the copy though? Why not throw it out?"

It was a question neither of us could answer.

"What do you know about the other guy Shelby was seeing?"

"Jesse? Not much."

"Did he come around?"

"I saw him twice. Once when she said they'd just met and one other time not too long ago. The second time I saw him, they'd been in a fight. I told Coop about him, and I'm sure he's talked to them already. I wanted to tell Cade about the fight, but I was worried he'd do what he did to Paul, so I didn't."

"What makes you say they were in a fight?"

"When he walked out of the guesthouse that last time, he slammed the front door. Then he got in his truck and peeled out of the driveway."

"Do you know why or what happened?"

"I'm not sure," she said. "After he left, I walked over to see if she was all right."

"What did she say?"

"All she said was, 'I'm fine, don't worry about it.'"

CHAPTER 18

The sun's rays bounced off the glistening snow, blinding me. I pressed my hand to my forehead, using it as a visor, and kept on walking. I was looking for a cluster of pine trees Maddie had described as "a mother and father tree with a baby in the middle." It didn't take long to find the snowy trio, or the rock where Shelby had been gunned down. I turned back, glancing in the direction I'd just come from. I could see Maddie's house and a couple of others on the same street. Shelby had been so close, and yet so far away at the same time.

In the distance, two children tossed snowballs at one another while their mother looked on, laughing and taking photos. Near the pond, a couple walked together, the man's arm slung around the woman, pulling her into him. The park appeared so safe and happy. It was hard to believe only a short time ago it wasn't.

I crouched next to the rock, smoothing the snow off the top with my hand, allowing my mind to drift back to the memories I'd shared with Shelby—the good times, the bad, the chance to be the positive role model she'd never had. She'd been stripped of life, and I'd been stripped of the chance to see the woman she would have become.

As far as suspects, we still only had two. I believed Elise had nothing to do with Shelby's murder, and even though she'd claimed to be with Paul at the time of the murder, I wasn't totally convinced of his innocence. Rage was rage. If he was capable of killing his wife in cold blood, he was capable of killing Shelby. I just needed to find a way to prove it one way or the other.

While I sat there contemplating, a shadow, long and black, spread across the rock like an eclipse of the sun. I wasn't alone. Someone was there with me.

I looked up at the large, crooked nose looming overhead and said, "Coop, what are you doing here?"

"We need to talk."

CHAPTER 19

W e've talked to every Adele Winters in the area," Coop said. "No one matched the age or description of the girl who visited you the other night."

We walked toward Maddie's house. "Maybe she's not from here, or maybe her ID was a fake."

He shrugged. "Or maybe you gave me the wrong name on purpose."

"Are you accusing me of lying?"

"Did you?"

I stuck my hands inside my coat pockets. "I've never been dishonest with you about anything."

"You've kept things from me. Same thing."

"It *isn't* the same thing. I've withheld information from you in the past because you do the same thing to me. You never tell me anything, never answer my questions, never—"

He raised a finger. "I got it. Stop squawking."

"You could have told me Nick works for you, you know, instead of springing him on me last night like you did."

He grinned. "And spoil the surprise? Why would I do that?"

We arrived back at Maddie's house, and he followed me inside. He lifted a baseball cap off his head, ran a hand through his graying hair, then stuck the cap back on again.

"I can't imagine you drove over to talk to me about the girl who visited me the other night, so why are you here?"

He seemed pleased that I asked. Too pleased. He took out his cell phone, opened a video, and flipped the phone around. He pressed play, and I watched as Maddie and I walked around the guesthouse earlier that morning.

"How did you ... where did you get this?" I asked. "Did you set up a surveillance camera in there?"

He nodded.

"Why? It's not the crime scene."

"We found a few cigarette butts on the ground outside of Shelby's bedroom window when we were gathering evidence. Maddie doesn't smoke, all of Shelby's friends we interviewed don't smoke ... well, not cigarettes anyway, and from what we know about Shelby, she didn't smoke either."

"She didn't."

At least I didn't think she did.

"It's possible the murderer watched her for a time, possibly waiting for the right moment to attack. We made a couple casts of the size-ten shoe impressions we found in the snow close to where Shelby was murdered. We found the exact same prints outside of Shelby's window. They weren't preserved well enough to cast, but they appeared to be the same tread pattern. It was a long shot to set up the camera, but hey, looks like the long shot paid off, just not in the way I thought it would."

Maddie's slender frame cast a shadow across the floor in the next room. I assumed she was leaning against the wall, listening. She stepped into the room and said, "I ... uhh ... just made a pot of coffee, if you're interested."

"Black," he said. "No sugar. And don't think you're off the hook, Madison. I told you to stay clear of the guesthouse."

"Uhh, the way I see it, you set a camera up on my property without my permission, so if you're going to point a finger, you'd better point one at yourself too."

She turned, disappearing into the kitchen.

"I'd like to call a truce," I said. "I don't know why you released Cade instead of charging him, but I appreciate it. Besides, we can cover more ground if we work together."

He extended his hand, palm facing me. "Not interested. I'm just here to get what I came for."

I moved a hand to my hip, knowing what he wanted—the wooden box. "You're a bitter, arrogant ass."

"Excuse me?"

"Whenever our paths cross, you're a complete jerk. I don't know if it's because I'm a woman, or if it's because you have a problem with me in general. I don't care what authority you have now. I'm done trying to get along with you. I just wish every case wasn't such a nightmare. You hate me. I don't know why, but hey, it's fine. I accept it."

I expected a verbal lashing, one of his usual quick-witted comebacks, crushing words meant to put me to shame. Instead he blinked, said nothing. The rewarding victory I'd hoped to feel for putting him in his place didn't come. I folded my arms, and we stood in awkward silence.

He sighed. "Well, I've been meaning to do this, and I guess now is as good of a time as any. I want to show you something."

He pulled his wallet out of his pocket. "Let's sit."

We walked into the living room, and each took a seat. He peeled back a stack of twenty-dollar bills in his wallet and removed a photo. It was bent and creased—worn, like it was older than the wallet he carried it in. He smoothed it with a hand and then offered it to me.

I stared down at the photo in disbelief. "Is this your daughter?"

He nodded.

"I can't believe it," I said. "She looks like ... *me*."

Her hair was long and a couple of shades lighter, but her more delicate features—the shape of her face, the sparkle in her deep brown eyes, her tiny lips—all mirrored mine.

"She did look like you, yes," he said.

"Why didn't you tell me before?"

"I didn't feel it was any of your business."

"Why are you telling me now?"

He shrugged. "What you just said about me hating you ... it isn't true. You're not my favorite person, but I don't hate you."

I got it now. "It must be hard for you to be around me. When you look at me, you must think of her."

"At times. It isn't just the similarity in looks. Your mannerisms, your attitude, putting yourself in danger and taking unnecessary risks—she was the same way. The past is the past. I don't like to think about it. I don't like to be reminded of it either."

"You're not the only one with a past you'd rather forget. We all have things that cause us pain."

Maddie entered the room, passed around the cups of coffee, and sat down, crisscrossing her legs on the couch. "Nice to see the two of you bonding."

"I wouldn't call it bonding," Coop said.

She changed the subject. "What did you get out of Paul? Anything?"

"Not a thing," Coop said. "He's still playing the insanity card. Met with his lawyer today, and the lawyer ordered a psych evaluation."

"He's *not* crazy," I said.

"Oh, I know he's not," Coop said. "He can play his games. Won't matter. He'll end up in prison either way."

"I sent Shelby's autopsy report to you a few hours ago," Maddie said. "Have you looked it over yet?"

"Yep. It's useless. There's no usable evidence. No fingerprints. No sign of sexual assault. Nothing to help us catch this guy." He looked at me. "And that's why you're going to give me the box I saw in the surveillance video."

I went into the next room, removed one of the business cards from the planter base, and took the box to him. He handed his coffee mug to me like I was his personal assistant and said, "Thanks, I gotta run."

CHAPTER 20

I found Jesse Baldwin, installing sheetrock on a framed house in a new subdivision on Cranston Drive in Murray. He was tall and slender, with rosy cheeks and short, tidy, blond hair. He had an innocent farm boy look about him, like he hadn't uttered a curse word in his entire life.

I introduced myself, and he seemed to know why I was there. Another detective had visited him earlier. I assumed it was Nick.

Jesse set his staple gun down on a piece of plywood and suggested continuing the conversation in the model unit, which I appreciated. I was shivering, and the model was heated. A few minutes later, after I'd thawed out, he started the conversation.

"I can't believe what happened to Shelby," he said. "It's a darn shame."

"When did the two of you meet?"

He thought about it. "About five weeks ago, I guess. I was walking out of the gym after a workout and she was coming in. She dropped her water bottle, and I picked it up. I told her I'd give it back if she agreed to have lunch with me."

"What did she say?"

"She smiled and then said yes. The next day we went for a drive. I know this spot where deer group together and thought she'd enjoy seeing some wildlife. We had a great time. I couldn't get enough of her laugh. I can still hear it, like she's standing beside me."

"How much time did you spend together?"

He walked to the kitchen and opened the refrigerator. "You want anything? Let's see … we have a few root beers in here and some lemon-lime soda."

"I'm fine."

He grabbed a donut off the counter, cracked open a root beer, and took a few swigs. "I saw Shelby off and on, whenever she had free time. In the beginning, we were together a lot, almost every day. By the third week, it started to change."

"What happened?"

"She was always busy. I tried talking to her about it, and I didn't get anywhere. She kept making excuses about why we couldn't go out."

"What changed? Do you know?"

"She didn't say. I came second to whatever else she had going on in her life. I tried calling, she wouldn't answer. Hours would go by. Sometimes she'd call back. Other times I'd get a text message the next morning saying she'd fallen asleep. The first couple of times, I let it slide. Then I felt like it was one excuse after another. I figured if she couldn't make me a priority, I wasn't sticking around."

"Did you talk to her about it?"

He nodded. "Sure did."

"What did she say?"

"Not much. She wasn't much of a talker. I figured she was blowing me off for someone else."

"Did she mention anyone else?"

"She said I was the only one she was seeing. I wanted to believe her, but when I saw her leaving a hockey game with two of the players, I knew she was hiding a part of her life from me. One of the guys took her to his car, and after she got in, he leaned down and they kissed. It wasn't a peck on the cheek either."

"What did you do?"

"I waited at her house until she came home, and then I confronted her. She tried to say the guy was someone she'd dated before she met me. She only agreed to go out with him again so she could break things off. I knew I was being fed a line of crap. I'm not an idiot. I know when I'm being played."

"Did she ever mention a man named Paul to you?"

He shook his head. "She never talked about anyone else, not even her friends. Seemed kinda weird."

"How did it end between you?"

"We went to a movie one night. Halfway to her house she got a text message, and then she asked me if I could turn around and drop her off at a friend's house."

Finally I was getting somewhere. "Where does the friend live?"

He gave me the address, an upper-class neighborhood in Capital Hill.

"Did she happen to mention whose house it was?"

"She didn't. I dropped her off, we kissed, and she watched me drive away before she went inside. I thought it was strange since it was so cold outside, but honestly, the entire relationship was strange."

"Did you see her again after that night?"

He nodded. "Right before she died, actually. I went to her house, told her I couldn't be involved with her anymore. I said I wanted a committed relationship, something that was going somewhere, and I didn't think she wanted the same thing."

I crossed one leg over the other. "How did she take it?"

"She teared up. But you know something? I didn't feel like her tears were for me. I don't know. Hard to explain, I guess. She seemed lost, like she wanted to be with me, but at the same time she didn't."

The front door opened, and a man poked his head in. "Jesse, you gonna finish working today or what?"

"I'll be right there," Jesse said.

"I have one last question. Did Shelby ever mention having any problems with anyone, or seem worried about anything?"

He shook his head. "I know it's not the answer you want. And look, I heard about the article in the paper. It explains a lot. Makes me wonder what else she was hiding. Figure that out, and maybe you'll find the man you're after."

CHAPTER 21

Knowing I needed to repair the damage I'd done with Nick, I sent him a text and asked if he wanted to take a ride with me. He agreed, and I drove to his house to pick him up. I parked curbside and let him know I was there. Everything about him seemed different now. I was shocked to see him living in a stucco house in a cookie-cutter neighborhood, and owning of a fat, gray cat, which was perched atop a sofa, staring out the window at me like I was tonight's dinner.

The front door opened, and Nick stepped out. A woman followed after him. She smiled at me as she walked him to my car.

Great, just what I need right now, an awkward exchange with my ex-boyfriend's wife.

She was everything I wasn't—younger, thinner, innocent, and she had a sweet, fresh face, like she hadn't experienced a day of hardship in her entire life.

Nick opened the passenger-side door and bent down. "Sloane, this is my wife Marissa."

Marissa leaned in and extended a hand toward me. I shook it.

"I hope you don't mind me coming out here like this," she said in a thick Southern accent, "but Nick has talked a lot about you, and I really wanted to say hello."

I was unclear about her true motive for meeting me. Wanting to keep the conversation brief, I went with a standard reply. "Nice to meet you."

"Can I just say something? I really like your short hair. Looks great on you."

I resisted the urge to say—*thanks, not everyone can pull it off.*

And by everyone, I did mean her.

"Thanks."

"I think what you do for a living is really neat," she said.

Neat?

Good grief.

Again, I thanked her, hoping the compliment part of our conversation was over, and we could wrap things up and be on our way.

But no ...

She said, "Oh, and I'm sorry to hear about your ... well, I guess she was like your step-daughter, right?"

I smiled at Nick in a way that prompted him to look at Marissa and say, "We need to get going, honey."

Yeah, honey. We need to go.

"Oh, okay," she said. "When do you think you'll be back?"

"I don't know. I'll call you if I'm going to be too late."

She glanced at me for a split-second and bit her lip, and I saw the worry in her eyes. She may have been more sugar and spice than I could handle, but I didn't feel right about leaving without putting her at ease. "I just need him to talk to a suspect with me. We won't be long."

My words seemed to pacify her. She brushed her lips across Nick's and backed away from the car.

Halfway down the street, Nick shook his head at me. "I see the judgmental look on your face, Sloane. What are you thinking?"

"She seems a little on the young side."

"Do I detect a hint of jealousy in your voice?"

"You detect a hint of honesty in my voice."

"Marissa's not that much younger than I am."

"Not much is relative. I'd guess she's at least eight years your junior."

"Seven. She's in her mid-thirties. Why does it matter?"

"It doesn't."

He strapped his seatbelt on and moved the seat back. "What do you need?"

"I wanted to apologize about the other day."

"You drove over just to say you're sorry?"

"Partially. I'd like to blame my outburst on all the stress I've been under since Shelby's death, but I can't. I shouldn't have made the assumptions I did. You've changed. You seem different now, and I can tell she makes you happy. I'm glad."

"I feel like a different person now. I know I didn't always handle things the right way when we were together. I was overbearing at times. You deserved better."

"I wasn't perfect either. I think breakups give us an opportunity to be better, and sometimes that means better for someone else."

"What about you? Are you happy? I mean, were you, before all of this happened?"

I considered the question. "Yeah, I was. I mean, I still am. Cade is good for me."

"I'm glad. I want you to be happy."

"I was thinking, if you're still open to working together, I have a couple of tips to pass along."

He nodded. "Shoot."

We discussed my meeting with Jesse Baldwin, and then I told him about the house Shelby went to on Capitol Hill.

"Yeah, he told me the same thing when I saw him earlier. I've been sitting on the information for a minute."

"Why?"

"Because I know whose house she was at in Capitol Hill, and given what we know now about what Shelby did for a living, I've been trying to decide the best way to approach it."

"Whose house is it?"

"Clinton Presley's. He's a Utah state representative."

I shook my head. "Figures."

"We might as well talk to him. Let's take a drive to his house and see what we can find out."

Minutes later, we stood on the porch of a turn-of-the-century mini-mansion. The front door opened, and a portly woman in her early fifties wearing a white suit jacket and a matching skirt smiled and said, "Nick, it's good to see you."

"Hello, Rebecca. How are you?"

"Very well, thank you. We're off to a choir concert at the tabernacle."

She looked at me. "And who's this?"

"This is Sloane Monroe. She's an old friend of mine."

Before I could speak, a man rounded the corner. He was thin and statuesque, everything the woman was not.

"Rebecca, can you help me with these cufflinks?" He walked into the foyer and noticed us standing on his porch. "Oh, Nick, good to see you. We were just about to head out for the evening. What are you doing here?"

"I need a minute or two, if you can spare it."

Clinton looked at Rebecca. "How are we doing on time, honey?"

She glanced at the watch on her wrist. "We have about five minutes."

We were invited into an office decorated in floor-to-ceiling mahogany, wine-colored velvet curtains, and bookshelves filled with antique books. Rebecca disappeared into another room, leaving the three of us alone to talk.

"What's this about?" Clinton said.

"I'm guessing you heard about Shelby McCoy, the college student who was murdered in the park this past week," Nick said.

Clinton leaned against the wall, crossed one leg over the other. "Sure, I heard about it. How's the investigation going?"

"Slow. I'll get right to the point. I'm here because we received a tip."

Clinton wiped his brow. "Oh yeah? What kind of tip?"

"We were told she was dropped off here, at your residence, sometime in the last week or so."

Clinton reached out and pushed the door closed. He glanced at me. "I'm sorry, who are you?"

"Sloane Monroe. I'm a private detective. Shelby was my boyfriend's daughter."

His eyes widened.

My admission had unnerved him.

It had also given him away.

Nick leaned in, lowered his voice. "We know Shelby was

working as an escort, Clinton. I need to know why she was here."

"I'm not sure what to say except your tipster was wrong. There are several homes on this street. What makes him so sure it was mine?"

"We were given your address."

Clinton shrugged. "Still doesn't mean your informant was right."

"He also described the house," I added. "Yours is the only one with five white columns across the front."

The clack of high heels headed in our direction, and the conversation paused. Clinton's five minutes were up. Rebecca opened the door and leaned toward her husband. "Sorry to interrupt, but if we don't leave now, we'll be late, and we're sitting right up front."

Clinton looked at Nick and then at his wife as if he were trying to determine which was the lesser of two evils. "You'll need to leave without me, honey. There's an important matter I need to discuss here. I'll join you shortly."

She frowned. "But if you're late, it will be hard for you to—"

"I'll hurry."

"Well, all right then. Don't be long."

"Okay, dear. I won't."

We waited until she pulled out of the garage, and Nick started up again. "I'm paying you a courtesy by coming here. I could bring you in, pass you off to Coop, and expose whatever extracurricular activities you've been indulging in. We've known each other for a long time, and I consider you a good man. I'd prefer not to do that."

"You couldn't possibly think I could have anything to do with—"

"I'm offering you the chance to keep your dignity," Nick said. "So why don't we cut through the bullshit? Tell me what I want to know. Shelby was here. Why?"

Clinton walked to his desk, unlocked the bottom drawer, and removed a bottle of scotch. He tipped it toward us. "Either of you care to join?"

I shook my head.

Nick nodded. "I'm off the clock at the moment. I'll indulge in one drink."

It surprised me, but if a little camaraderie put Clinton at ease, I was all for it. Clinton poured a shot's worth of scotch in a glass, handed one to Nick, then poured the same for himself. He walked to the window and looked out. "My wife doesn't know I drink."

I had a feeling his wife didn't know a lot of things.

Nick joined Clinton. "Let's talk about Shelby, so you don't keep Rebecca waiting all night."

Clinton swallowed the scotch down in one gulp and poured himself another. "I was meeting a few gentlemen in Las Vegas for the weekend and wanted a companion."

I bit my lip, which did nothing to contain my sarcasm. "Why not take your wife? She's a companion."

"These guys I take trips with on occasion ... we're all a member of the same club, meaning, we're all married, we all love our wives. Surrounding ourselves with young, classy women every now and then helps relieve the pressures of our jobs. It's all innocent fun. We'd fly everyone out to Vegas, relax, have a great time, and return refreshed, ready to face our daily routines again."

I wondered what all was included in the "great time" package.

"Shelby accompanied you on these trips?" Nick asked.

"A few times, yes." Clinton looked at me. "And just so you know, it wasn't about sex. I didn't sleep with her. I've never cheated on my wife."

He had a loose interpretation of what the word *cheating* actually meant.

"And the other men?" Nick asked. "Did they have sex with their dates?"

Clinton shrugged. "Not my business, and I don't see how it's relevant."

"How often did you see Shelby?"

"A few times over the past year. She was a good girl—bright and funny—easy to be around, easy to talk to about anything. I could say whatever was on my mind, and she didn't judge me."

"Did she ever talk about her personal life, ever seem worried or act like she might be in danger?"

Clinton shook his head. "Every time I saw her she was happy and lighthearted. She didn't seem to have a care in the world."

Nick folded his arms. "I need to know where you were Monday morning between six and eight."

"Oh for hell's sake, Nick. Really?"

"I have to ask."

"Actually, you *don't* have to ask. You *know* me. You know I'm not capable of murder."

"I thought you were a loyal, happily married man with three children, and yet today, you shocked me."

"I love my family. I'm a good husband and a father. I thought if I explained everything you'd understand. Guess you don't."

"You didn't answer my question about where you were the morning Shelby was murdered," Nick said.

"I'm where I am every weekday morning at that hour—in my office at the capitol building. My secretary will vouch for me. Are we done here?"

"Almost. I need the name of the agency you used to hire Shelby."

Clinton shook his head. "Sorry, I can't give you that."

"If you don't want your wife finding out about your fun little side trips, you will."

"You don't understand. I signed an agreement. I'd be putting myself and my colleagues at risk."

"Not my problem," Nick said. "If you don't tell me what I want to know, I will talk to your wife."

"You wouldn't."

"Try me."

"I thought we were friends."

"We are," Nick said, "and as your friend, I'm asking you to help me out."

"I'll be blacklisted, banned forever." Beads of sweat formed on his forehead. He wiped them away. "If I tell you, you'll keep my name out of it, right?"

"If I can."

"You have to, Nick. Please."

"I want to believe you didn't have anything to do with Shelby McCoy's murder."

"I didn't."

"As long as I have no reason to consider you as a suspect, whatever you say right now stays in this room."

Clinton sighed. "Fine. It's called Play with Me."

"Excuse me?" I asked.

"Play with Me. That's the name of the escort service."

"I need an address and a number," Nick said.

"I don't have an address." He walked to his desk, pulled a sticky note out of a drawer, scribbled down the number and a website URL, and handed it to Nick.

"How does it work?" Nick asked.

"You go on the website. Log in with the name UtahEscorts and the password Ready2Play. Choose the girl you want and book the date and time. Call and make the payment, and that's it. I wouldn't use your real name, if I were you. They have a list of all the law enforcement around here."

CHAPTER 22

Nick ran a search on the company and came up with a physical address. It took us to a small office downtown where it didn't appear any business was actually being conducted. The letters *PWM Incorporated* were on the outside of the building, but the lights were off, the door was locked, and after a quick look through the front window, it was obvious no one had been there in some time.

Nick explained the business cards found in the planter box I'd given to Coop were worthless. He had tried the number, only to discover the line was no longer in service and attached to an untraceable burner phone.

We queued up plan B, returning to Maddie's house and using her computer to log in to the business's private website. We clicked on the gallery of girls and scrolled through their profiles. There were eleven in all, most of them dressed in skimpy clothing and posed in such a way that their faces were hidden from the camera. I didn't see Shelby. I also didn't see the girl who had called herself Veronica.

"I'm thinking we should just pick one of these girls and make the call." Nick pointed at the computer screen. "What do you think about this one?"

"Hang on. Some of these girls look soft and some look hard. We're more likely to get what we're after with one who's nice."

He backed away from the computer. "Okay then. You choose."

I leaned in, taking a second look at the photos, and then pointed at a girl with long, blond hair, bright blue eyes, long legs, and a wide smile. "What about her?"

He nodded. "Krista it is."

Nick made the call, posing as an executive in need of an evening companion. He requested Krista's services and was quoted an hourly rate of two hundred twenty-five dollars. The booking agent who took the call said she'd check with Krista about her schedule and call back. Four minutes later, she did, and the meeting was set.

"I should go alone," Nick said.

"No way. I'm going."

"I just think it would be better if I—"

"Nick, I'm going."

A short time later, we waited in a fancy hotel room in Park City that was scented with an aroma of pine and vanilla. Krista arrived right on time. I hid behind the door while Nick answered it. She walked in, set her purse down on the table, and removed her jacket. She folded it over a chair, caught a glimpse of me, and jumped.

"What is this? What's going on? I don't entertain couples."

"This isn't what it looks like." Nick pulled a chair out from under a small table. "Take a seat, and we'll explain everything."

She did what he asked.

I stood in front of her, "I'm in a relationship with Shelby McCoy's father. I believe you knew her?"

She crossed one leg over the other, nervously fidgeting with the hem on her tiny black dress. "I didn't know her very well. What do you want?"

"The name of the woman you work for, and an address."

She shook her head. "I'll lose my job."

"Not if we don't reveal how we found out."

"I ... I don't know."

I leaned in close, my face inches from hers. "We need the name of the woman you work for, and you're going to give it to us."

Nick glared at me like I needed to back down, so I stepped away, waited for her answer.

She brushed a tear off of her cheek and said, "You think we can help you, and we can't. None of us can. We don't know who killed Shelby. My boss called a meeting right after she found out what happened. She talked to us, and then she talked to all of Shelby's former clients. No one knows anything."

Or someone was lying.

"I'll make you a deal," Nick said. "Tell us who you work for and how we can find her, and I promise to leave your name out of it."

"I don't know you. You can say whatever you want right now."

Nick pulled out his credentials and handed them to her. "My name is Nick Calhoun, and I'm a detective working on Shelby McCoy's case. Please, we need your help. You can trust me."

She rubbed her trembling hands together in her lap, considering his request. "Okay, I guess. I work for Delia Monahan."

"And where does she live?"

She paused and then said, "Not far from here, actually."

CHAPTER 23

A brisk wind whistled through the city, piping damp moisture into the cool night air. I reached for the zipper on my coat, closed it around me, and knocked on the door. Seconds later, a girl answered, her eyes wide with recognition.

She squinted and then crossed her arms. "*You.*"

For a moment I was too stunned to reply, overcome with shock that someone so young owned such a thriving, provocative business. It didn't seem possible, but here she was. Nick looked at the girl and then at me, confused.

"Ahh … do you two know each other?" he asked.

"This is the girl who came to see me the other night—the one whose name we've been trying to figure out."

"The one who called herself Veronica?"

I nodded.

She moved a hand to her hip. "How did you find me?"

"It doesn't matter. We're here now, and we need to talk."

"No," she whispered. "I need you to leave. You can't be here."

"We're not going anywhere, Delia. It *is* Delia Monahan, right? You have some explaining to do."

She attempted to push the door closed, but Nick wedged a shoe inside, stopping her.

"I can't talk to you," she said. "Not right now. I ... I'll come to your friend's house later. Any time after eleven o'clock. Pick a time and I'll be there."

"The time is right now," Nick said. "There is no later."

A woman descended the stairs, joining Delia at the door. She was around my age with long, auburn hair, piercing blue eyes, and milky-white skin. "Can I help you?"

I pointed at Delia. "We're here to talk to Delia."

A look of confusion spread across the woman's face. "She's not Delia. I am."

I pointed at the girl. "If you're not Delia, who are *you*?"

The girl blinked, said nothing.

"This is my daughter, Adele," Delia said.

Her *daughter*. Her underage daughter. The ID I'd seen had been a fake—same first name, fake last.

Adele and Shelby must have been friends. When Shelby died, Adele wanted to warn me about what she knew while protecting her mother's identity in the process.

Impatient to get the answers we were after, Nick said, "Ma'am, I need to talk to you about Shelby McCoy."

Delia shrugged. "What makes you think I know anything about her?"

"We know about the business you're running. We also know she worked for you as an escort."

I expected Delia to flinch, deny it, or do something rash.

Instead she held up a finger, indicating we needed to wait. Turning to her daughter, she said, "Adele, go start on your homework while I talk to our guests. I'll be up to help you in a few minutes."

"I want to stay," Adele said.

Delia shook her head. "Do what I ask."

Adele nodded and Delia swung the door open, motioning for us to come in. "Follow me to my office, please."

Delia turned and led the way while Adele skulked down the hall beside us. I squeezed her shoulder and leaned in close.

"Don't worry. I won't say anything," I whispered.

She breathed a sigh of relief, mouthed the words *thank you* and ascended the stairs.

Once we entered Delia's office, Nick dove right in. "We went by your place of business earlier today. It doesn't look like you've operated from there in a long time."

She shrugged. "There's no need. Most of my business is conducted over the phone. I can book appointments from anywhere."

"Why bother with a storefront then?"

"We use one of the rooms as a photo studio to keep the girls' profiles updated. The other we use for storage. Anything else you would like to know, Detective Calhoun?"

"You know who I am?"

"I make it my business to know everyone in law enforcement." She turned toward me. "But I don't know you. Why are you here?"

I explained.

"Why did you act like you didn't know Shelby just now?" Nick asked.

"I never said I didn't know her. I was feeling the two of you out. I have a lot of paperwork to get to tonight, so if you wouldn't mind, let's get to your more pressing questions."

"All right, fine," Nick said. "How long had Shelby been working for you?"

She glanced up. "Let's see now ... she started midway through her first year at college. She was referred to me by another young woman who used to work for me."

"I know," I said. "Heather Farnsworth. She died last year."

"Yes, I'm aware. I was sorry to hear it."

"Did Shelby ever mention having problems with any of your clients?" Nick asked.

She shook her head. "Shelby was one of my most popular girls. She was well liked. If anyone had mistreated her, or anyone else, I wouldn't have hesitated before turning him in to the police. I have a zero-tolerance policy where the girls' safety is concerned. Fortunately we cater to the kind of men I don't often worry about."

"I'm going to need a list of all of the men who hired Shelby," Nick said.

She shook her head. "It's not possible."

"Why not?"

"No personal records are retained—not here or at the office."

He scoffed like he didn't believe her. "Fine. If you want to play it that way, I'll get a warrant, but I *will* see those files."

"I invited you into my home, Detective, even though I was under no obligation to do so. Get your warrant if you must. It won't change anything. After we screen a client, and their time with the girl they've hired has concluded, we incinerate any information we've collected to protect their privacy. Essentially, there's no database or list of past clients."

"You're lying," he said.

"If you have a problem accepting what I'm telling you, I'll give you my lawyer's card, and you can take it up with him."

"What can you tell me about Paul? He was one of Shelby's regulars. We understand he was in love with her."

"Like I said, I'd be happy to give you my lawyer's information, but I won't be speaking to you about any of my clients."

We'd hit a wall, and it was clear nothing we said would penetrate it.

"I guess we're done here then, for now," Nick said.

"Not quite," she said. "Since you're here, there is one detail worth sharing. Shelby came to me before she died. She thought someone was following her."

"When did this happen?"

"Last week."

"Why haven't you notified the police?"

"Because I have no specific details to report. Without concrete information, what good would it have done? Shelby never actually *saw* anyone following her. She didn't even know whether it was a man or a woman. My girls are squirrely enough after what just happened, and I have a business to run. I can't have them thinking their next client might be a gun-toting Boogey Man looking to end their life."

Nick pulled a card out of his wallet and handed it to her. "Here's my number. If anything changes and you have reason to believe any of your girls are in danger, contact me."

"Understood." She turned toward me. "I'm sorry about Shelby. She was a sweet girl. I was very fond of her, as was my daughter."

On our way out, I asked one last question. "What made Shelby feel like she was being watched, did she say?"

"It was a feeling she had—the kind of feeling we all get when we're alone and every hair on our body stands up on its own. We may not know why our body reacts the way it does. We just know something is wrong."

CHAPTER 24

At four o'clock the next morning, Maddie and I began the trek back to Wyoming to attend Shelby's funeral. While I drove, Maddie leaned a pillow against the window and slept. I sipped on an energy drink, using my mind to keep me company. I processed everything I knew about Shelby's murder so far, which wasn't enough. I couldn't shake the feeling I was missing something—something big, something I hadn't thought of yet.

I'd been working on the assumption that Shelby's murder had been motivated by someone in her own life, in her circle of friends, or in the industry she worked in. Now I questioned that logic. In all my years as a private investigator, I had always considered myself a good judge of character. So why did I have the feeling none of the characters I'd questioned so far were guilty?

Paul.

Elise.

Jesse.

Clinton.

It felt like I was standing amongst a group of trees, barking. No matter which tree I chose, it was always the wrong one. The escort angle was an easy one to latch on to, and I had assumed Shelby's murder was tied to it somehow. Now I was starting to feel like her death had nothing to do with the business she was in. The pieces weren't coming together like they should. There was a different path I needed to follow, perhaps one that hit much closer to home, and I just needed to find it.

CHAPTER 25

The funeral home was packed to overflowing, with latecomers being forced to stand outside the service in the crowded foyer. I sat on a pew in the front row with Cade, my hand clutching his. At the far end of the row, Shelby's mother sat next to a man twice her age. He was grossly overweight and wearing a button-up shirt with half of the top buttons undone, exposing a gray, hairy chest no one wanted to see and couldn't unsee once they did. In the looks department, he was a flat zero, but Wendy was with him for his money. Based on the gold chain dangling around his neck and the diamond watch adorning her wrist, he had plenty of it to go around.

One look into Wendy's glassy eyes and it was obvious she was using again. Her last stint in rehab had been due to an addiction to cocaine. I wondered what her drug of choice was this time.

The sermon started with a prayer that lasted so long it felt more like a speech. It was followed by Cade's cousin singing a mediocre yet heartfelt rendition of James Taylor's *You Can Close Your Eyes*. Then it was Bonnie's turn. She delivered a touching address and showed a slideshow she'd put together with photos of Shelby throughout the years.

Next up was Cade.

He made his way to the front, faced the crowd, and stood there, tall and stoic, searching for the words he wanted to say but couldn't bring himself to do it.

A minute passed.

Then two.

We locked eyes, and with the slightest shake of his head, I knew he couldn't go through with it. He stepped down, and I stood up, searching for the words Cade would have me say.

"I knew Shelby for the last few years," I said. "In that time, I watched a rebellious teenager blossom into a beautiful, confident woman. One of my favorite memories was watching her tease her dad. She used to hide behind the corner and wait for him to come around, and then spring out in front of him. No matter how many times she did it, she still managed to surprise him."

I went on for the next several minutes, doing my best to say some of the things I knew Cade felt in his heart. And then came time for the inevitable—I passed the torch to Wendy.

Wendy adjusted the front of her short, spaghetti-strap dress and walked to the podium, her slip-on wedge sandals clicking against the heels of her feet with each step. I exchanged looks with Bonnie, who was poised on the edge of her seat, ready to jump up if necessary. It wasn't our first rendezvous with Wendy—we'd attended a funeral with her before. When it came to Wendy's unfiltered mouth, it was best to prepare for the worst.

"I wasn't the best mother," Wendy began. "I didn't braid Shelby's hair or read her bedtime stories, or make sure she brushed her teeth at night, but I loved her as much as any woman loves her child. She was a good girl, and she was smart. She was going to college so she could do something special with her life."

She paused, patting a hand against her chest as if to calm herself. So far she'd come off beautifully, but the longer I gazed upon her face, the more I detected a shift in her demeanor. The tide was about to change, and we would all be swept up in its wake.

"My baby girl was murdered. Shot. Someone ended her life, some savage, and now he's out there running around, free to do it again to someone else's precious daughter. Why isn't anyone talking about that? Why isn't anyone doing what needs to be done to find the bastard and end his life?"

Bonnie and I stood at the same time.

"Enough!" Bonnie said. "This is your child's funeral, Wendy. Don't make a scene."

Wendy swished a hand through the air. "It's okay. It's okay. I get it. Y'all think I'm crazy, but you want to know what I think, standin' here, looking out at all of you, all prettied up in your Sunday best, trying to have a respectable service, pretendin' what happened is fine? It's not fine. It will *never* be fine. Save your condolences, your sympathy for my loss. I don't need 'em."

After her "drop the mic" moment, she walked up the aisle and out the back door. Her boyfriend followed behind like a faithful puppy. The pastor cleared his throat and walked back to the podium, doing his best to smooth over what had just happened. He led the congregation in a song and then ended with a prayer.

I looked at Cade. "You all right?"

"Why'd she have to ruin it? Why'd she have to make a fool of herself today of all days?"

"She's dealing with what happened to Shelby in her own way. It's not the right way, but it's the only way she knows how."

He let out a long, tired breath. "I don't feel like talkin' to anyone right now. I just wanna get out of here."

I slid my hand inside his. "Why don't we head to the truck and sit for a few minutes before we drive to the cemetery?"

He nodded, and we stood, walking together toward the back door. A few people reached out along the way, patting him on the arm, giving him a smile. Cade's puffy, swollen eyes hid the tears he wouldn't let fall. He focused on the ground, never lifting his head until we reached the back door. He pushed it open, and we stepped out.

A loud bang pierced the air, the sound of a gun being fired at a relatively close range. My head whipped around as if in slow motion, processing what had just happened, even though it seemed more like a dream than reality. I squinted, focusing in the direction the sound had come from. A man in a ski mask, dressed head to toe in black, darted out from behind a vehicle, pausing a few moments to meet my gaze before running toward a tree-lined hillside behind the building.

I was too stunned to move, my feet planted on the ground like they'd been strapped to weights. I turned toward Cade, blinking in disbelief as the present moment came into focus again, and the awareness of what had just happened hit me. Cade had been shot, blood dripping from his forehead onto his suit. He glanced at me and then released my hand, his body slumping to the ground.

I fell to his side, hovering over him, screaming.

CHAPTER 26

Running—the sound of the man's feet hammering into the pavement as he made a swift getaway. The moment after he'd squeezed the trigger, he'd stood, holding Sloane's attention for several seconds while she stared him down, trying to understand what had just happened and why. She had probably been in shock. Shock that gave him the upper hand, the time he needed to pop up from behind the car and make his escape before everyone else exited the building.

He took refuge on a hillside next to the funeral home, the perfect place to watch the aftermath unfold. He reached into his bag and removed his binoculars. Time to assess the damage.

The shot he'd taken was a good one, but had it been good enough to do the job he'd intended? With the mass number of human bodies swarming around Cade like bees protecting their hive, it was impossible to tell whether he was alive or dead.

He scanned the area, focusing the binoculars on Sloane. She stood in front of Cade, looking around in a daze. A man walked up to her, grabbed her arm, and pulled her away from Cade. They talked for a moment, and then she raised a finger, pointing in the direction of the hillside. Given the distance, it was unlikely she would be able to make him out very well, if at all, but he knew it was only a matter of time before she made her move.

That's right, Sloane.
Follow me.
Take the bait.
You know you want to.

CHAPTER 27

Maddie pushed her way through the crowd of funeral attendees, trying to get to me. Cade's fellow officers split into two groups, two providing cover around Cade, and the other two ushering everyone back inside the funeral home for safe keeping.

I flashed back to the moment I'd locked eyes with the masked man. He was tall and muscular. Even with the mask over his face, he seemed familiar somehow. And he'd stood there, waiting, like he *wanted* me to see him, *wanted* me to know he was there.

Why?

Maddie knelt in front of Cade, assessing the bullet wound and checking for a heartbeat. "I feel a pulse. He's alive, for now, but he's losing too much blood too fast. I need to get pressure on his head wound."

I felt someone tugging on my arm and whipped around. Quaid Hooker, the ME in Jackson Hole, and one of Cade's best friends, grabbed me, looking me over from top to bottom. "Sloane, are you okay? Were you hit?"

"I'm … yes. I mean, yes, I'm fine. No, I wasn't hit. Cade was the only one who was shot."

"What happened?"

Part of it was still a blur.

"We were … ahh … walking to the truck," I said. "I heard a shot go off. I didn't know what it was at first until I looked over at Cade, and his head … he was … it was bleeding."

"Do you know the direction the shot came from? Did you see anything?"

Did I see anything?

Yes.

I *had* seen something.

"I saw a man in a ski mask, running. No. Wait. Before that. The man shot Cade and then jumped out from behind one of the cars in the parking lot."

"Which car, do you remember? And where did he go?"

I closed my eyes, replayed the last few minutes in my mind, and then looked in the direction he'd gone. I saw something up there, in the trees. Something shiny. Was he there now, watching?

"There," I pointed. "He's there. He ran up the hillside."

Hooker glanced in the direction I was pointing.

"I need you to help Maddie with Cade," I said.

While Hooker alerted the officers to what I'd just said, I set off in a sprint, crossing the parking lot, and entering the thicket of trees where the masked man had gone minutes before. I stopped, glanced at the snow, quieting my mind.

Focus, Sloane.

See what you need to see.

I found a set of footprints and took off running again.

Footsteps crunched through the snow behind me—someone approaching fast. I glanced back. Detective Proctor and another officer or two were on my heels. Proctor was a small, squatty man who made up for his lack of height in muscle mass.

He could chase after me if he wanted.

I wasn't stopping.

"Sloane, wait up," Proctor shouted. "Slow down!"

I reached the place where I thought I'd caught a reflection of something and canvassed the area. Footprints circled around me, spreading in every direction, like the shooter had run around, attempting to throw me off.

Proctor caught up to me and grabbed my arm. "Hang on a sec, Sloane. Let's talk. Hooker said you saw the shooter up here. That right?"

I nodded, pointing at the shoe prints in the snow. "See all of these?"

"Yeah."

"When Cade was shot, the man ran in this direction. And I could have sworn I saw something shiny, reflecting from up here."

He inspected the footprints. "Most of these are too smeared to really give us an idea of where he went next. Powder's not packed enough either. Still, I'll get a couple of the guys out here right away."

"I think we're dealing with the same person," I said, "the one who killed Shelby."

"How can you be sure?"

"These tracks might not be intact, but the size is in line with the prints Maddie found at Shelby's crime scene in the park. Plus, the coincidence ... Shelby then Cade?" "Huh, okay. Let's hold tight for a minute."

He made a couple calls.

The steady whine of an ambulance sounded off below, and my thoughts turned back to Cade. I was torn. His life was on the line. I regretted taking off like I had, especially now when the man we were after was nowhere to be found. I could have waited. I should have waited.

"I should be with Cade," I said. "I should ride with him to the hospital."

"Yeah, you should," Proctor said.

I couldn't tell if he meant it or if he was just trying to get rid of me.

I called Maddie.

"How is he?" I asked.

"I'm going to give it to you straight. He's a mess, Sloane. I was able to stop the bleeding for the most part. I won't know how bad he is until we get him to the hospital and he gets checked out. The ambulance is loading him up now."

"I'm sorry I took off."

"Where did you go? Where are you?"

"I saw the guy who shot him run up the hillside, and I followed. His footprints are everywhere, but he's gone. I'm coming down. I should be with Cade."

"He's unconscious, Sloane. He won't know the difference."

For now.

"If he wakes up and I'm not there—"

"What would Cade want you to do? Think about it.

Think about what he'd do if this happened to you."

He'd want to stay with me, but if he'd seen what I had, he would have gone after the killer too.

"Stay up there and see what you can find," Maddie said. "I'll ride over with Cade and meet you at the hospital in a few."

I slipped my phone into my coat pocket and said to Proctor, "This was a premeditated attack. Someone waited in the parking lot for Cade to come out."

"Just like someone waited for Shelby to walk home that day," Proctor said. "The shot was dead on, and in my opinion, clearly meant to target him and not you. What I'd like to know is …"

He trailed off, his focus shifting from me to something else.

"What is it? What are you looking at?"

"I'm not sure. You mentioned seeing something reflective up here. Think I know what you were talking about."

He pointed.

I looked.

Dangling from a branch of a tree several feet away was a piece of black fabric about the size of a credit card. The back was coated with reflective tape.

"Stay put while I check it out," he said. "Might be nothing, might be something, might be a trap."

He walked to the object in question. Before touching it, he ran his hand along the ground, locating a twig. He snapped it in half, using it to poke around before removing his camera phone and snapping several photos.

"Well, what is it?"

"The one side is nothing more than a strip of fabric. Cotton, looks like."

"Maybe a piece of his coat got caught on the branch when he was trying to get away."

Proctor shook his head. "Nope, it's much more than that. He left this here for a reason. It was planted. He wanted us to find it."

"How can you be sure?"

He motioned for me to walk over. I did.

"Take a look at this," he said.

Attached to the fabric was a playing card, this time a Jack of Hearts. Written on the card was a message: *How does it feel to lose the one you love?*

CHAPTER 28

A larger picture was forming, one wherein revenge proved to be the guiding force behind the shootings. New questions entered my mind, pushing me in a different direction.

What was the game the killer was playing, and why?

And what was the real meaning behind the message on the playing cards?

I thought about Cade's history in law enforcement. Over the years, there had been times when firing his weapon had been his only option. There had been fatalities. Not many, but a few.

Could the loved one of someone Cade had killed be seeking justice?

If true, why had the killer waited until now?

It didn't make sense.

I found Maddie pacing the waiting room floor of the hospital. We made eye contact, and the look on her face gave me pause, scaring me. Whatever news she was about to deliver, I believed it wasn't good.

"Glad you're here," she said.

"Is it bad? Just tell me. No matter how hard it is, I need to know. Is he …"

Dead.

I choked on the word, unable to get it out.

"He's alive, Sloane, and he's in surgery. That's the most important thing you need to know right now."

I breathed hope into my lungs. "What aren't you telling me?"

"Everything should be fine. There is a chance he might not make it through surgery, but so far he's doing all right. I spoke with the neurosurgeon. He's a friend of Hooker's. He has performed this type of surgery before, and he's optimistic he can save his life."

"What do you know so far?"

"When we arrived, he was still unconscious and in critical condition, but the good news is the bullet went through and through. If it had lodged inside his brain, we'd be looking at a much more severe injury. He probably wouldn't have survived the trip to the hospital."

I dug deep, focusing on the positive—hope instead of fear.

Cade was tough.

A fighter.

He would survive.

He had to survive.

"Tell me about the surgery they're performing," I said.

"The operation is called a decompressive hemicraniotomy."

"A what?"

"It's a lot to explain. We don't need to go into the specifics of it right now, okay?"

I shrugged. "Why not? I want to understand the procedure."

"If I go into detail, I'm afraid you'll freak out."

"Why?"

"Because it sounds a lot worse than it is. To be frank, it sounds crazy, but it's not."

I crossed my arms in front of me. "Tell me. I want to know."

She walked to the reception desk, asked for a piece of paper, a pen, and a clipboard, and then walked back over to me. We sat down, and she drew me a picture—a cartoonlike version of a brain.

Using the pen as a pointer, she said, "Okay, so, let's say this is Cade's brain and this is the area where the bullet hit. The neurosurgeon needs to remove a portion of the skull to allow his brain to expand."

She was right. It did sound crazy, reminding me of the scene in *Hannibal* when Hannibal had removed Krendler's prefrontal cortex. "Why does it need to expand?"

"To lower the pressure in his skull."

"There's pressure in his skull?"

She grabbed my hand. "The important thing to remember here is that it needs to be done in order to keep Cade alive."

"What happens to the part of skull they remove?"

"They use a computer to recreate the shape of the piece of bone that was removed, and they make a plastic replacement."

"And when the surgery is over, will he be fine? Will he be normal again?"

"No, Sloane. He won't. Probably not for a long time. He'll need to work with specialists to recover the functions he lost. But the good news is, Cade's a fighter. If anyone can come out of this, he can."

CHAPTER 29

Several hours later, Cade was out of surgery. He'd survived, but was still considered to be in critical condition. The surgeon disallowed visitors, at least until the following day when he could reassess Cade's condition. I didn't like it, but I understood.

Nick arrived in town for a meeting Proctor had set up. Proctor hoped merging details about the case would help us create a better profile of the killer. We met at Cade's house, filing into the den for a group discussion. Before we got started, Nick called Coop so he could listen in via phone.

Proctor began by saying he'd spent the day sifting through Cade's old case files. In his opinion, we were looking for someone with a vendetta against Cade. We needed a connection—any connection—to tie Cade's attempted murder to someone from his past. The question was whether or not we'd find it.

"All right," Proctor said, "let's get started. I've got Hooker at the lab going over the forensic evidence. He'll be checking in with me if he finds anything of interest."

"My friend Maddie is also there assisting him," I said.

Proctor's jaw tensed. "Yes, I heard."

"Is that a problem?"

"He needs to focus and not get distracted. She can stay, for now, as long as she doesn't get in the way."

"Get in the way?" Coop snorted through the phone. "She's one of the top medical examiners in the country. She'll be the one assisting *him*, not the other way around."

Proctor frowned, looking irritated. "Getting back to why we're here, Cade is usually in charge of cases like this, but I've been asked to step in. Based on the playing cards left by the killer at both crime scenes, the perp is sending a clear message. It's safe to assume he's out for vengeance and has a bone to pick. We need to find out why."

"The calling card is key," Nick said. "First the Ten of Hearts, and now the Jack. He's working up to something."

"A royal flush," Coop said, "which means he's only hit two out of five targets. How are you profiling him?"

"I believe the man we're looking for is either a criminal out for revenge, or a member of the criminal's family, looking to do the same thing," Proctor said. "Both attacks were planned, methodical. He's somewhat organized and disciplined. The words '*how does it feel*' suggest rage, and I'd even say resentment."

"I agree," Coop said. "The window between the first attack and the second was small. It won't be long until there's a third. You have any good suspects?"

"For now I'm focusing on two of his old cases."

"Why only two? Seems a bit on the slim side, if you ask me."

"We can expand from there. My strategy is to isolate suspects who have reason to retaliate against Cade and work outward from there, most likely suspects to least."

"What's your plan?"

"I'll be speaking with the suspects' families to see if I can find a connection."

"I assume you're giving us permission to speak to them as well?" Coop asked.

Proctor sighed. "You know, I understand what you're asking, but it would be better for you to let us handle the—"

"I don't think so. We're either working together or we're not. I didn't send my man up there so he could sit on his ass while you do the dirty work. He's there to get dirty, and I'm expecting you to let him."

"He won't be sitting around," I said.

"Wasn't asking you, Sloane," Coop said.

"Your man was asked here for a reason," Proctor said, "We're doing our best to cooperate."

"Good, that's all I wanted to know. I've got someplace I need to be," Coop said. "Nick, I'll give you a call later for an update."

"Will do," Nick said.

Nick pressed the end button on the phone.

Proctor shook his head. "Geez, is he *always* like that?"

"For as long as I've known him," I said. "Be grateful you only had to deal with the mild version. It could have been a lot worse."

He raised a brow. "Well, we'd better discuss these suspects."

Proctor grabbed a folder on the coffee table and flipped it

open. "First up is Jeff Ward. He was incarcerated ten years ago for killing a female store clerk during an armed robbery."

"What made you choose him?" Nick asked.

"He's always claimed he is innocent."

"How can he be innocent if a woman was killed?"

"The robbery involved Jeff and his cousin Ned. In Ned's original statement, he said Jeff had pulled the trigger, and since Jeff's prints were also found on the gun, Jeff received the lion's share of the prison sentence. For years Ned stuck to his story. Then last year at his parole hearing, he broke down, said Jeff wasn't even in the store at the time of the robbery. He now claims Jeff was the getaway driver, which was what Jeff had said all along."

"What does Jeff claim happened?"

"In Jeff's statement, he said it was supposed to be a robbery, nothing more, and that Ned had told him there weren't any bullets in the gun—it was just for show. Ned shot the clerk, ran out of the store, handed Jeff the gun, and told him to hide it. Jeff shoved it under his seat. Seconds later as they were making their getaway, cops caught up to them. The gun was taken into evidence, and the only prints found on it were Jeff's. Not a single one belonged to Ned. In Jeff's defense, he said Ned must have wiped the gun clean before handing it off to him."

"What prompted Ned to change his statement?"

Proctor shrugged. "No idea. He just did. Bawled like a baby, said he was ashamed Jeff had received a life sentence that should have been his. We talked to his cellmate, and he said he'd been quoting scripture lately, claimed to have found Jesus."

"Where is Jeff now?"

"He was released a couple months ago. Lives a few miles from here in a rundown house on the edge of town. Word is he's been looking for work, and no one will hire him."

"If he wanted revenge for all of those years spent in prison, why not just go after Cade and spare Shelby?"

"Hard to say what goes on in these bottom-feeders warped minds. Time served may have jacked his brain."

I saw his point, but wasn't convinced. "Who's next?"

Proctor closed Jeff's folder and opened the next. "Margot Wiggins."

It was a name I was familiar with—one Cade had mentioned every now and then. "I know about her. She's the one who held her ex-husband hostage when he wouldn't hand over the kids."

Proctor nodded. "You're right."

"What's her story?" Nick asked.

"She lost visitation rights with her two youngest boys because of her drug addiction," Proctor said. "A week out of rehab, she showed up at her ex-husband's house all hopped up on cocaine, toting a gun, ready to blow his brains out."

"What happened?" Nick asked.

"When she drew on her husband, Cade did his best to talk her down, but when he realized she was going to shoot, he had no choice. He fired."

"When was this?"

"Couple years ago."

"Did she survive?"

"She was in a coma for a while, until her parents made the decision to take her off life support."

I shook my head. "If she's dead, how could she be a suspect?"

"She isn't the suspect," Proctor said. "Her oldest son Joe is. He was overseas when she died, in the Army. I hear he's back now, came home last month. Rumor is he blames Cade for what happened. He's been going around town saying Cade could have spared his mother's life if he wouldn't have shot her where he did."

"Cade hesitated," I said.

"What do you mean?" Nick asked.

"Right before he shot her. He was going for her shoulder, trying to disarm her with the least amount of damage, but he aimed too high. He still loses sleep over it, even though he was justified in what he did. If he wouldn't have taken the shot, her ex-husband would probably be dead."

"I know that, and you know that," Proctor said. "But her son refuses to believe anything other than the story he has created in his mind."

I sighed. "Which suspect are you talking to first?"

"Think I'll start with Jeff and Ned. I want to hear their stories myself."

I nodded. "Care if I take Nick and see what we can get out of Joe?"

He rubbed his hands together. "If I say no, are you going to do it anyway?"

He knew me too well. "Probably."

My phone lit up, a text message from Bonnie giving me an update on Cade.

"Everything all right?" Nick asked.

I nodded. "Yeah, Bonnie's just talked to the surgeon. I should call her."

Proctor checked his phone as well. "Looks like they've recovered the bullet. It lodged into the wall at the funeral home. Found the casing, too, behind one of the cars."

"Was it a Speer Gold Dot Centerfire?" I asked.

He nodded.

"We're dealing with the same perp, but just to be sure, I'll have Hooker run a comparison on the marks on the casings and the bullet's ridges and valleys, even though we all know what we're going to find."

"The question is, who is he targeting next?" I said.

Proctor slid his chair back, stood, "Since you mentioned it, if the killer is picking off those close to Cade, I assume you're on the list. I'd like to put a detail on you."

It had been on my mind all day—the constant looking over my shoulder, wondering if the killer was out there, watching and waiting just like he had with Cade and Shelby. One thing I questioned: If Cade was the one he wanted to make pay by having those around him suffer, why not save Cade for last?

"Put a detail on me if you like, but I can take care of myself. I always have a gun on me, and I'm keeping an eye on my surroundings."

"Still, I'm putting a couple guys here at the house."

"I'm here too," Nick said. "I won't let anything happen to her."

Proctor slid his fingers into his pockets and sighed. "I get what you're both saying, but don't you think Cade would have said the same thing? And look where *he* is right now."

CHAPTER 30

Joe Wiggins was lean and tall, six foot five or so, with dark, greasy hair that looked like it hadn't been shampooed in quite some time. His face was long and oval and had a hollow, sunken look to it. But what stood out the most was a distressed tattoo of an eagle taking up half of the real estate on his forearm.

I stood at the door with Nick, ignoring the fact that Joe was eyeballing me like he was the biggest rat in New York City and I was the prized cheese.

"Who are you?" he grunted.

"My name is Sloane Monroe, and this is—"

"I don't care 'bout your name, lady. Who *are* you?"

Nick stepped forward, taking over the conversation. "We're investigators here working on the—"

"Wasn't talkin' to you, man." He pressed the tip of his fingertip to my nose. "Was talkin' to her. You single?"

"I'm almost twice your age."

"So what? You single or not?"

"Whether I am or not doesn't matter."

He grinned, leaned against the doorframe. "Maybe it should."

A frustrated Nick looked like he was seconds away from giving Joe's face a makeover. We were getting off topic.

"I'm a private investigator working on Cade McCoy's case," I said.

He jerked his head back, laughed. "That asshole? Don't waste your time. Looks like he got what was coming to him. Doesn't surprise me. I knew he would sooner or later."

I tightened my jaw to keep from spouting off, and then dove back in, switching gears. "I'm sorry about what happened to your mother."

He shook his head. "Don't be. It's in the past. I don't think about it no more."

"How are your younger brothers doing?"

"Fine as two kids can be without a mother."

"Your father doesn't have anyone new in his life?"

He rubbed a hand along his jawline. "What do you want from me, really? I mean we can stand here forever, shooting the breeze. Why not just tell me why you're here?"

"We're looking for the guy who shot Cade," I said. "We were hoping to ask you a few questions."

He curved his lips into a smile. "*You* can ask me anything you like, but I don't know anything about it other than what I've heard."

"Can we come in?"

Joe stepped back, allowing us inside his quintessential bachelor pad.

A musty smell of burnt pizza and sweaty socks wafted through the room, so strong I wished I'd remained outside, even though at half past ten in the morning, it was a brisk twenty-two degrees. Joe swept his hand across the sofa, pushing a pile of newspapers, biker magazines, and fast-food bags to the floor.

"My maid is off today," he laughed. "Have a seat."

"Over the last week, Cade—"

Before I could finish, he cut me off.

"Just hang on a second. First things first." He headed to the kitchen, grabbed a few beers from the fridge, and set them down on coffee table. "Want one?"

We refused. He shrugged, cracked one open, and plopped down on an old, tattered chair that was torn in multiple places. He leaned back, spread his legs, and got started on the beer. "Okay, continue."

"I was saying, Cade McCoy's daughter, Shelby, was murdered in Salt Lake City this last week, and yesterday there was an assassination attempt made on Cade's life."

"Yeah, so?"

"You just returned from the military last month, and I hear you've been going around town telling everyone you blame Cade for your mother's death."

"Yeah, and? I have no reason to lie about it."

His tone was calm and pensive. If I'd rattled him, it didn't show.

"Your mother was going to shoot your father," I said. "Cade was just trying to do his job. If he could have spared her life, he would have. Believe me."

He finished his beer and opened a second one. "*Believe you*? Really? I know why he did it, but he could have taken a different shot. Not only did he kill her, he did it right in front of my brothers. Far as I'm concerned, he's dirty—as dirty as a cop can get."

"He's not, Joe. He still thinks about what happened that day. He didn't want to shoot her at all."

"How would you know?"

"I just do," I said.

He leaned back, kicked his bare foot on top of the coffee table. "Yeah, well, she's dead, and ain't nothin' gonna change it now. No use talkin' about a past that can't be changed, right? I mean, what's the point?"

"The point is, Cade's in the hospital, struggling for his life," Nick said. "And when we put together a list of suspects who have reason to take a shot at him, you're at the top."

"Well, ain't that convenient? I didn't shoot him, or his kid. I'm not a murderer. I wouldn't be sittin' here talking to you without reprehension if I had anything to hide."

By reprehension I assumed he had actually meant to say representation, but I didn't see the point in correcting him. I leaned over, snatching a deck of playing cards off of an end table. "Mind if I take a look at these?"

"Keep 'em if you want. I have more."

I pulled the cards out of the box, fanned them out, and counted. All there. Next I divided them into suits. Again, none were missing.

"Do you own a firearm?" Nick asked.

"Uhh … this is Wyoming, man. Who doesn't?"

"Answer the question."

"I own three, and they're all registered. You can check."

"What kind?"

He told us. Given we knew the type of bullets used, none of his guns matched the one we were after.

"What kind of gun was used in the shooting?" he asked.

"We can't discuss that information," Nick said.

"'Course not."

"Where were you yesterday around noon?"

"With my brothers at Tony's Pizzeria."

"How long?"

"Long enough. Ask anyone who works there."

"Where did you go after you—"

"Okay, guys," Joe said. "I see where this is going. I'm not stupid. You think *I* shot him. I already said I didn't. Karma bit him in the ass yesterday, and I feel no sympathy for what happened to the guy. But I didn't shoot him, and I wouldn't shoot a woman. Anyone who would doesn't have his head straight. You two can show yourselves out."

CHAPTER 31

I sat across from Nick at a local coffee shop, eating a chocolate-filled croissant and blowing on my chai latte to cool it down. "Well, what do you think?"

"Hard to know what to think anymore," Nick said. "I don't think Joe is responsible for what happened to Shelby or Cade. Sure, he ran his mouth, but he seems far too lazy and stupid to orchestrate something like this on his own."

"We're zero for two again then. Proctor doesn't think Jeff Ward did it either. I feel like the intuition I usually get is just not there. I'm blocked."

"When we were together and you couldn't figure something out, you used to do yoga. Most of the time it worked. You'd get clear again."

"I haven't had the time."

"Maybe you should make some."

I left him and drove to the hospital, not knowing what to expect when I arrived. Turned out Cade was heavily sedated, in a coma-like state. The nurse said it was a necessary step, helping to rest his brain.

I wandered through the halls, not knowing what to do or where to go. I thought about what Nick had said about getting clear and went in search of a chapel. It was a small room with two rows of chairs. A cross was nailed to the wall at the front. It was crooked, and I was about to walk up and fix it until I noticed a woman sitting in the first row. Her eyes were closed, hands pressed together in prayer. She uttered some words under her breath and then opened her eyes and looked over at me.

"I know who you are," she said. "You're Sloane."

I nodded. "Who are you?"

She planted a wooden cane on the floor, using it to help her rise, and then walked over and sat in the chair next to me. "I've known Cade since he was a boy. His father and I were close friends. I wasn't sure whether they'd let me see him today, but I thought I'd come down and try. How are you doing? Are you okay?"

No. I wasn't.

"I'm trying to be."

She glanced back at the cross and smiled. "You know, in times like these, I find prayer is one of the only things that brings me comfort. Are you religious?"

I shook my head. "Not really. I believe in something, a higher power perhaps. I'd like to believe in some form of afterlife, that when we die, we go on, existing in another way. I just don't know for sure."

"I can tell you're troubled. Not just about Cade—about a lot of things."

"I've never been so frustrated with a case before. I'm trying to find the man responsible for what happened to Cade and Shelby before he strikes again. Everything's cloudy, and I need it to be clear."

"You've been through a lot, hun. You can't expect a cloud to separate before its time."

She was right.

She tapped me on the leg, stood. "Clouds and darkness surround us, yet Heaven is just, and the day of triumph will surely come, when justice and truth will be vindicated."

"What an interesting quote."

She winked. "Yes, it is. A wise quote from a wise woman. It was Mary Todd Lincoln who said it. Good luck to you. I have no doubt you'll find the man you're looking for when the time is right."

She walked through the doorway and disappeared into the hall. I remained for a moment, leaning back on the chair, thinking I'd close my eyes and give clearing my mind a shot. But even then, all I could see was the crooked cross, taunting me to walk to the front of the room and do what came naturally. So I did.

It was possible I was keeping myself from becoming clear, knowing clarity would force me to face a single truth I wasn't ready to accept, about who the killer might really be after. Before I could give it any serious thought, I heard a voice in the hall. Maddie.

"All right, all right. I'm fine!" she said. "I don't need your stupid chair. It's just a flesh wound. Stop forcing your agenda on me, mmm ... kay?"

I found Maddie and Hooker standing in front of a nurse,

who was determined to put Maddie in a wheelchair. "Maddie? What's going on?"

She looked over. "Oh, hey. I was just going to call you."

I looked her up and down. "What happened? Why is there blood all over your shirt?"

"Uhh, well, there's a simple explanation. I've been shot."

CHAPTER 32

The man balled his hand into a fist, punching it against the cabin wall, again and again and again. He'd shot at Maddie and missed his target, and not by a small margin, by a lot. To make matters worse, before he could get off another shot, she had pulled herself back inside the building and locked the door behind her, making it impossible for him to finish what he had started.

He was slipping, making careless mistakes, botching what should have been an easy kill. He slumped onto the bed, sinking down into the mattress. The springs poked into his spine, needling him like they too were reminding him of his failures. He snatched a half-full bottle of whiskey off the nightstand and tipped it back, guzzling it down until it was gone. He hurled it, watching it shatter against the log walls.

He needed to rethink his game plan, and fast.

He'd hit Cade where he'd intended, but somehow, Cade had survived. And with the 'round-the-clock surveillance outside of his hospital room, there was no chance of getting close to him anytime soon. Maddie would also be protected.

He knew what he needed to do, to keep his focus on what mattered most, his endgame. There was only a small timeframe in which to acquire his next target, and he couldn't fail, not this time. She was the key to everything.

CHAPTER 33

"You were *shot*!" I said.

Maddie boosted herself onto a patient bed and reclined back. "Yeah. It's no biggie. Hurts like hell though."

"When did it happen, and where?"

She shrugged. "Hooker and I were at the lab. We decided to break for lunch. I walked out first, and he was grabbing his coat and meeting me at the car. When I got outside, I looked over and noticed a guy standing there. He was dressed in black with sunglasses and a ball cap, and he had his arms crossed in front of him. It looked like he was waiting for someone. I assumed he was one of the assistants' boyfriends until he jerked one of his arms forward, and I realized the jackass was holding a gun."

"Did he say anything?"

She shook her head. "As soon as I saw the gun I backpedaled. He fired. I pulled the door back open, got back inside, and locked the door. Then I yelled for Hooker."

"Did the guy come after you?"

"Yeah. He advanced on me and tried to get into the building. I ducked into one of the offices and hid behind a desk until Hooker found me."

"How bad is the wound?"

She lifted her shirt, exposing a blood-soaked bandage over her chest. "You ask me, it's kinda hot. I mean, think about the stories I can tell now when I'm on a date. I'll have one hell of a scar. And hey, guys dig that shit."

"Maddie, this isn't a joke. The guy could have killed you."

"I know, but hey, the dude didn't hit a major artery. I'll be just—"

She stopped, realizing the gravity of the word she'd almost said. She'd be *fine*. Shelby and Cade hadn't been so lucky.

She leaned back on a pillow and looked up at me. "I'm sorry, Sloane. The rush of adrenaline is making me ignorant."

I placed a hand on her shoulder. "Don't be. I'm glad you're okay. Were you able to get a good look at the guy before you went back inside the building?"

She shook her head. "It all happened so fast, I wasn't able to focus on any of his features. I've thought about it, but it's just a blur. He had the cap pulled down as low as it would go over his face, and it was too hard to see his hair ... anything really. He was hunched over when I first saw him, but even then, I could tell he was tall. I know it's not a lot, but it's something, I guess."

Hooker entered the room and was followed by a nurse. He'd caught the tail end of Maddie's words and added, "After I found Maddie and she told me what happened, I took off outside, but the guy was long gone by then."

The nurse went to work on Maddie's wound. She suggested it might be better if we left and returned later, adding something about the hospital's policy on visitors. Maddie furrowed her brow, saying she didn't give a damn about proper procedures. The nurse grunted something under her breath and left the room.

I sat in a chair next to Maddie's bed and organized my thoughts. If the killer had only been interested in those closest to Cade, Maddie didn't fit the bill. He would have gone after someone closer to him, like me, or one of Cade's closest friends or other relatives. Another theory came to mind. It was possible the killer's target was Hooker, but when Maddie walked out of the lab door first, the killer had no choice but to shoot her once she saw him. This didn't gel with me either. The killer was methodical, his attacks premeditated and planned. He wouldn't get sloppy now.

Maddie snapped her fingers. "Earth to Sloane. What's going on over there? Are you listening to me?"

"Sorry, what did you say?"

"It's not important. What are you thinking?"

"I'm trying to figure out why you were the target."

She shrugged. "Maybe he was after Hooker. He *is* Cade's best friend."

"I thought that too at first, but nothing in his MO leads me to believe he shot you by accident. We're missing something here. *I'm* missing something."

And I was beginning to understand what it was.

"I don't know, Sloane. None of it makes sense." She pointed to her backpack on the floor. "Hey, can you hand me my bag? Actually, I don't need the whole bag, just my cell phone. Coop called. I told him I'd call him back."

I unzipped the top of her bag and looked inside. "I don't see a cell phone in here."

"Oh, you know what? I think I put it in one of the side compartments. Sorry. Try the left pocket. It should be the only thing in there."

I unsnapped it and reached inside, pulling out a phone and handing it to her.

"There's something else in here too."

I stretched the pocket out and peeked inside.

"Well, what is it?" Maddie asked.

I lifted the item out of the pocket, holding it up in front of me. Between my two fingers was a playing card, the Queen of Hearts, and written on it, a familiar message: *How does it feel?*

"The bullet *was* meant for you, Maddie. You were the target."

"But why? Why me?"

I just shook my head, because I didn't dare say what I was thinking—not until I was absolutely sure.

CHAPTER 34

A few hours later, I was standing in Bonnie's living room trying to decide what I wanted to say, or if I should be saying anything at all.

Noticing my inner tension, she started the conversation. "How's your friend Madison doing?"

"She's fine. I wanted to talk to you about something."

Bonnie nodded. "Of course, dear. Go on."

"I believe everyone is being targeted because of me. What I mean to say is, I believe I'm the one the killer is truly after. I wish it wasn't true, and I wish I had a better explanation, but I don't. After what happened to Maddie today, it makes sense."

"Have you shared your opinions with anyone else?"

I shook my head. "Not yet. You're Cade's closest family. I thought I owed it to you, to tell you first."

"Even if what you're saying is true, as hard as it is to accept, it's not your fault."

"Sure it is, Bonnie. If I hadn't been in Cade's life, Shelby would be alive right now, and Cade wouldn't be in a hospital bed struggling to survive."

Although I could see the pain in her eyes, she managed a slight smile. "You can't predict how it would have altered their reality. None of us can. Do you honestly think Cade hasn't made enemies over the years? And look at the life Shelby was making for herself. She was an escort, for heaven's sake. Every choice we make in this life has a risk attached to it—a consequence—and sometimes those consequences are out of our hands. Besides, you're not sure whether your theory is even true or not yet."

But it was true—I could feel it.

"If it turns out I'm right, I want you to know how sorry I am."

She wrapped her arms around me. "I'm not interested in an apology, Sloane. You're not the one who needs to give it. I do need you to do something else for me though."

"Anything."

"Get yourself right in the head so you can find the man who did this and bring him to justice. If you don't, and he gets away with what he's done, not only will you spend the rest of your life looking over your shoulder and worrying about all those you love, I fear you'll never get past this, and it will consume you for the rest of your life."

CHAPTER 35

I woke to find Nick sitting on my bed, his hands gripping my arms, shaking me awake. The lamp on my nightstand had been switched on, the light beaming so brightly I stuck a hand out in front of me to shield my eyes. "What's going on? Did something happen? Is Maddie okay?"

"She's fine. She's asleep."

"Why are you in here then?"

"Your cell phone keeps ringing."

I looked at my phone. It wasn't lit up. "I don't think it was my phone. I would have heard it. Maybe it was something else?"

"It's your phone, Sloane. I know your ring tone. Honestly, I don't know how you slept through it. I could hear it from the living room."

Odd.

"Really?"

He nodded.

I sat up, rubbed my eyes. "I ... I'm sorry. I took something to help me sleep."

"Geez, whatever it was, it must have been strong. You were completely out."

After spending so many restless nights tossing and turning, unable to still my mind long enough to get the rest I needed to think straight, I'd had enough. I blinked my eyes a few times, trying to kick-start my engine. It didn't help. Every cell in my body begged me to return to sleep.

I grabbed my phone and clicked it on. Nick was right. I had three missed calls, all of them within the last ten minutes.

"Who has been calling you?" Nick asked.

"Annie."

"Who's Annie?"

"My gran's next door neighbor."

"Cordelia's neighbor?"

I nodded. "She's in her eighties, close to Gran's age, I think."

"How's Cordelia been? Must be about five years or so since I saw her last."

"She's the same spunky, high-strung woman you remember. Still has more energy than I do too."

"Is she still living in Park City?"

I nodded. "I usually drive down one weekend a month and we have brunch together. I'd leave on a Saturday, stop in and see Shelby, and then go stay the night at Gran's, and we'd go to Sunday brunch."

"It doesn't make sense that her neighbor would be calling you at such a late hour. You better call and see what's going on."

My limit for receiving bad news had reached max capacity. Annie wouldn't call unless she had a good reason. I put the phone on speaker and dialed. It rang a few times, and then Annie said, "Sloane, I'm so glad I reached you. I apologize for the late hour."

"It's all right, Annie. What's going on? Where's Gran? Is she okay?"

"Well, I don't know. I think so."

"What do you mean?"

"I can't get in touch with her just now. She's in Las Vegas, you see. I've tried calling several times, but she's not picking up. You know how she is when she gets around a blackjack table— she can go all night, and she always switches her phone off."

I had a vague memory of Gran telling me about an upcoming trip to Vegas. With all of the recent events happening in rapid succession over the last week, it had slipped my mind.

"When is she coming back?"

"I talked to her yesterday. She said she was leaving this morning, but she wouldn't be driving this early."

"I'm sorry, Annie. I still don't understand. Why is it so important for you to reach Gran right now?"

"Well, that's what I wanted to talk to you about. It was the strangest thing. About an hour ago, I woke up completely parched. I went to the kitchen to get a glass of water, and I noticed there was a light on at Cordelia's house."

"In which room? Is it possible she left a light on and you're just noticing?"

"No, no. This was an outside light. One of those motion-detector things, you know? I went to the window and looked out, and that's when I saw him."

"Saw whom?" I asked.

"A hoodlum, lurking outside of Cordelia's house. He had his hands cupped over his eyes like he was looking through binoculars, and he was staring through her window. I think he was planning on robbing the place and was checking to see if she was there."

My hands were sweaty, shaking, making it a struggle for me to hold the phone.

Nick reached out, taking it from me. "Here, let me help," he said as he put the phone on speaker.

"Who's talking?" Annie asked. "Is it Cade? Sloane, are you still there? Are you listening?"

"I'm here," I said. "When you saw the man next door, did you call the police?"

"Not at first. I figured he'd be in and out of her place before anyone could get here, and I wasn't about to let him get away."

"What did you do?"

"As you know, my husband Jerrold died last year."

To keep her from embarking on one of her longwinded stories, I cut in before she had the chance to continue. "I know, and I'm sorry about Jerrold, Annie, but I need you to tell me what happened after you saw the intruder."

"Yes, well, if you would have allowed me to finish ... Cordelia bought me a .38 Special after Jerrold died. It's a pretty little thing too. I keep it in the glove box in my car. I went out to the garage to get it, and, well, wouldn't you know it, I realized I'd forgotten to take my car keys with me, so I went back into the house to get them."

Nick and I exchanged a discouraged glance, hoping she was nearing the point of her story.

"I opened my front door," she continued, "pointed the gun, and yelled at the man. I told him he had ten seconds to get off her property or I'd shoot."

"What did he do?"

"Nothing, at first. He just stood there like a big fat dummy. Well, guess he wasn't fat. Didn't seem like it to me, but anyway, it was cold outside, and I wasn't going to stand there all night, half-dressed, and try to have a conversation with a halfwit, so I started counting down from ten."

"And then?"

"Once I reached five, his right hand started to come up, and I could see he was holding a gun too."

"If it was dark outside, how could you be sure it was a gun?" I asked.

"When he tripped the motion detector, the exterior light stayed on, and he was standing right beneath it. I saw that gun in his hand, and I told him if he even so much as lifted it another inch in my direction, I'd blow his brains right out the backside of his head. And would you believe it? He started laughing! It unnerved me to see some idiot with shit for brains standing there mocking me, so I showed him."

She *showed* him?

I could only imagine what was coming next.

"I put a bullet in his shoulder, and while he was bent over in pain, I said I used to be a police officer and went to the shooting range once a week. It's a lie, of course—well, the police officer part is—but I do go to the range with Cordelia all the time, and I'm a damn good shot."

"What happened after you shot him?" I asked.

"He ran off."

"Where?"

"Down the street."

"Did you see where he went?"

"He got into a car parked about five houses down."

"What kind of car?"

"I don't know. I didn't have my glasses on. The main thing is, he's gone now."

While she laughed into the phone, proud of her achievement, my heart sank.

He'd gotten away—again.

And he'd be back—again.

"Annie, did you ever call the police?"

"Sure, I did."

"And have they arrived yet?"

"They just walked in the door right before you called."

"Are they there now, in your house?"

She lowered her voice to a whisper. "Most of them are checking out Cordelia's property. Brought some fancy lights in so they could get a look at her yard. I asked why they bothered with such things. I mean the man's only an intruder, right? They refuse to give me any information. It looks like an alien ship landed over there. All of the neighbors on my street are awake, wondering what's going on. You're a private investigator. What do *you* think they're doing?"

For now, the less she knew the better. "Are any of the men from the police department in your house with you?"

"Yeah, one. And between us, he's getting on my last nerve. Smells funny too. Stinking up my house as we speak. And I don't care for his attitude either."

"Is his name Cooper?"

She paused and then said, "Yoo-hoo, policeman, what's your name, please? Hello?"

"Annie, did he answer?"

"Not yet. I think he mentioned his name when he arrived, but I was in a state, and now I can't recall. He's talking to somebody else. Gave me a lecture about all of the things I did wrong and what I should have done. I kept Cordelia's house safe, but does he care about that? Noooo."

"I'd like to speak with him," I said.

"Whatever for? I just told you what happened."

"Please, Annie, just put him on the phone."

"All right, fine."

I heard her walk over to him and say, "Excuse me, I have Sloane Monroe on the phone. She's Cordelia's granddaughter. She wants to talk to you."

"Tell her I need to speak with Nick," Coop said. "And I need privacy."

"Says he wants to talk to someone called Nick," Annie said. "Does that make any sense to you?"

"It does. Hand him the phone."

Nick took the phone off speaker, spoke to Coop for a minute, and then handed it to me.

"I want you back here," Coop said. "We need to get this mess figured out."

I sighed. "Cade's going to be in the hospital for a while. I haven't even been able to see him yet, and I'm worried about leaving before I have the chance to—"

"Now, Sloane. He has a long road to recovery. He'll still be there when this is all over. You can spend time with him then."

He was right, but it didn't stop me from feeling like a yo-

yo being tossed back and forth from one state to the other. I was tired of coming and going, tired of chasing dead ends. I was just … tired.

"You listening?" Coop asked.

"Yeah."

"How soon can you leave?"

"Couple hours."

"Make it one."

Ordinarily I was too feisty to be told what to do and when to do it, but my confidence tank was depleted. And he was right. In my current state, I stood a better chance at finding the killer with Coop by my side. "Okay, fine."

I ended the call, pulled my knees to my chest, and buried my head between them. I needed to think, but even more importantly, I needed to accept the horrible truth in front of me. I had assumed someone was around, watching me, keeping tabs on me and those close to me. I hadn't considered Gran might be a target. It was a mistake. A big mistake.

Nick sat on the bed next to me. "Sloane, hey, it's going to be all right."

"No, it isn't."

"Look at me, please."

I raised my head.

"It's not your fault. None of this is your fault."

He said the same thing Bonnie had said, but he was wrong. They both were.

"The truth has been right in front of me this entire time," I said. "And I didn't want to believe it. This was never about Shelby, and it was never about Cade. It was about me. It's been about me all along."

Shelby.

Cade.

Maddie.

Gran.

All victims. All have one person in common. Me.

They were targets because of something I'd done to offend someone else. I drank in the moment, let it all sink in, reflecting on the times in my life where two little words had sometimes crossed my mind: *What if?*

What if my line of work put those I loved in jeopardy?

Now it had.

Shelby was dead because of me. Cade was fighting for his life because of me. Maddie was shot because of me. And now Gran. I only hoped we found her before … I wouldn't allow myself to think it.

CHAPTER 36

I stood by Cade's bedside, watching him sleep. He looked battered and worn, thin—so thin and emaciated. It was like he was withering away. I leaned down and kissed his brow.

Nick poked a head around the corner. "Hey, Coop's asking if we're on the road yet. You ready?"

"I just need one more minute."

He nodded and left the room.

I'd hoped to have the chance to speak to Cade before I left, but I didn't want to wake him, so I leaned in and whispered, "I'm sorry about what happened to Shelby, and for what happened to you. If I had known being with me would have caused all of this, that I would have been the reason Shelby was killed, I would have given you up before anything happened between us."

"Is it true, what you said?" I turned, coming face to face with Wendy. "You're the reason my kid is dead? This psycho running around shooting people, it's all because of *you*?"

"I mean, we haven't caught him yet, so I don't really—"

She reached out, slapping me across the face. "Is it true? Well, is it? Answer me!"

Before she could hit me a second time, Nick stepped between us, shoving her against the wall and using his arm to restrain her.

"Nick, I'm okay," I said. "It's okay. We need to talk for a minute."

He stepped back, but remained between the two of us.

"I don't know if it's true yet," I said. "It looks that way."

She wagged a finger in the air. "I knew from the moment I met you that you were trouble. Tried to tell Cade too. He wouldn't listen. He was blinded by you just like everyone else. Not me though. You're nothin' but a stupid—"

Nick grabbed Wendy, shoving her toward the door. "You're finished."

"Not even close. This is between the two of us, not you. Mind your business."

"I'll put you in my car right now and drop you at the police station. I'm sure they wouldn't mind drug-testing you to see how much you've pumped into your system."

She stamped a foot onto the ground, huffing like a bull ready to charge.

"Get out of here," Nick said. "Go get yourself cleaned up."

Wendy flipped her middle finger and marched out of the room.

Nick turned toward me. "Enough of this, Sloane. I'm not going to stand here and watch you beat yourself up anymore."

"I deserve it though, Nick."

He shook his head. "This isn't like you. You're better than this. Tougher. Smarter. What would your sister say if she saw you like this right now?"

"This has nothing to do with her."

"Sure it does. Sam Reids murdered your sister. Then he came after you, came after your friends, targeting innocent women along the way. You found him and you stopped him. If you really want to help Cade and his family right now, let's catch this guy."

I couldn't save Shelby. She was already gone. I was weak, but I was also strong, the pain I felt quickly turning into something else—anger.

CHAPTER 37

I set a plastic file box down in front of Coop and popped the lid open. "All of my major cases are in here. They're arranged by year, and then in alphabetical order."

I expected the gesture to whet Coop's appetite and thought he would dive right in, but he didn't. He just sat there, staring at the files with an odd look on his face.

"Did you hear what I said?" I asked. "What's going on with you?"

He cleared his throat, grabbed a plastic cup full of water, swallowed it down, and handed the cup to Nick. "Would you get me a refill?"

Nick grabbed the cup, looked at me like he was just as confused as I was, and walked out of the room.

"Are you going to tell me what's going on?" I asked.

"You know earlier, when you were on your way back from Wyoming, and I told you we'd found your grandmother and she's okay?"

"Yeah?"

"Thing is, I needed you back here, not going rogue on me like you always do in these situations."

What was he saying?

"Where is she? Where's Gran?"

"We found her car. It was abandoned. Looks like she made it to Fillmore, stopped to get gas, and then … well, we're unsure of the rest. We searched the car. Her bags were still there, her purse, her phone. We're processing it now."

Even though I'd braced for the impact his words would have on me, it was like he was speaking in slow motion, every syllable of every word fighting to come through.

"Any witnesses? Did anyone see her?"

"The store clerk said she came in this morning, used the restroom, bought a bag of chips, and an iced tea. They had a short conversation, and she seemed fine. Surveillance shows her walking in and out of the store alone, and there was no sign of anyone suspicious lurking around."

Nick entered the room, placed the cup of water in front of Coop, and sat down. "What did I miss?"

Coop brushed a hand across his forehead and filled him in.

"What about the—"

"Playing card? A King of Hearts was taped to the steering wheel."

"What was written on it?"

He shook his head. "Nothing. Nothing at all. The good thing is our shooter has been killing on the spot. He didn't this time. I'm assuming he abducted her, which means he has a reason for keeping her alive."

"The *good thing*?" I said. "There's nothing *good* about this situation, Coop. You told me she was all right! You lied to me!"

"Directing your anger toward me isn't going to change the sequence of events. Wherever she is, I'll still find her, and I'll find him."

I bolted out of my seat. "No, *I'll* find her."

"Sit back down."

"I won't be ordered around. Not by you or anyone. I'm leaving."

"You need my help."

"Since when? You've never wanted *my* help, and you've certainly never asked for it except for when you're trying to get information out of me. You just want to keep me contained so I don't get in your way."

"This time is different."

"How? Because it seems the same to me."

"It's personal. We need to work together."

After all my previous attempts, I couldn't believe he was offering now.

"*Work together*? Why? You don't care about Gran. She's just a case you need to solve. I know you, Coop. I know how you operate. I don't need you to find her."

I flung the office door open and stepped into the hall, expecting Nick to jump up and try to stop me. He didn't. He let me go.

"You're right," Coop called after me. "Everything you said is true."

I didn't stop. I kept on walking. I felt trapped by him. I needed to break free.

Coop came into the hall. "Cordelia's not just a case, Sloane. And I do care about her on a personal level."

"Stop it, okay?" I shouted. "Stop doing this to me. You don't even know her."

"I do though. She's dating my father."

Dating his father?

I froze, trying to decide if it was true or just one of Coop's manipulation techniques. "Since when?"

"A few months ago."

"That's not possible. She would have told me."

"They met at a city fundraiser. Cordelia didn't know he was my father at first. When she found out, she didn't think you'd approve, given our history."

"You mean our rivalry?"

"I suppose now would be a good time to admit she's the one who suggested I show you the photo of my daughter. She said I needed to find some common ground with you, make things right, or she wouldn't agree to keep seeing my father."

I turned, looking him square in the eye. "I knew you had an agenda. You always do."

"Look, Sloane. Cordelia makes my father happy. So what if we butt heads all the time? You're a pain in the ass. I am too. We may never get along, but we can try, can't we?"

"How can you expect me to do that after what you just pulled?"

An elderly man stepped in front of me. He wore black-rimmed glasses and a bowtie, was a few inches shorter than Coop, and was dapper for a man of his age. He scowled at Coop and then stuck a hand in my direction. "Hello, I'm Alfred, Chief Cooper's father. You must be Sloane. I know how hard it is for you to work with my son right now," he said, "but please, for your grandmother's sake and mine, would you be willing to do it for me?"

CHAPTER 38

Over the past six years, I'd had a handful of high-priority cases, the kind where someone usually wound up dead. Vicki Novak had been killed by Coop, Sam Reids by Giovanni. A distraught Ivy West had thrown herself in front of a train. Eddie Fletcher and Shawn Hurtwick were both serving life sentences in prison with no possibility of parole. Rocco "The Rock" Romano had fled the country via plane only to discover he wasn't as clever as he thought. Giovanni had made it onto the plane with him, and while he had never been heard from again, and his body had never been found, it wasn't hard to imagine what happened to him. No one who crossed Giovanni Luciana had ever lived to tell about it. Rounding out my more recent cases, Rob Wilcox had taken his own life by shooting himself in the head. And finally, a jealous Carol Ayres was in prison for committing a double homicide.

Eight murderers.

Five dead.

Three in prison.

Coop divvied out the cases and questioned me about each one. Some he was already familiar with, and others he wasn't. No one stood out. We were looking for a family member connected to one of my cases who harbored enough resentment toward me to pick off the people in my life one by one. I didn't believe the man we were looking for was tied to my old cases. We were looking for someone else. Coop believed there was a good chance my hunch was wrong, but I knew it wasn't.

Who hated me enough to go after all those I loved? And why abduct Gran in? Given her car was parked in a public parking lot and there could have been people around, he may have decided it was better to wait. But that hadn't stopped him before, and I couldn't help but feel he had a grand finale planned—a finale that included me.

Even more curious was the way the killer had been discovered by Gran's neighbor. He'd tripped the outside light and then stood beneath it, almost as if exposing himself on purpose. Although Coop's men had been through Gran's house, I'd decided to take a look for myself.

Sitting on a folded blanked at the bottom of the bed in Gran's bedroom, I found her wedding album. I pulled it onto my lap and flipped through it. The last time I had visited, she'd pulled it out of a drawer, and we had spent half the day reminiscing about past memories. At the time I had wondered if there was a specific reason she was showing me the album that day. We'd gone through it together before. Had she planned on telling me about Alfred?

Nick and Maddie entered the room.

"How's it going?" Nick said. "Find anything?"

I shook my head. "You should be home with your wife. Not here with me. I'm sorry."

"She understands. Besides, if I weren't with you, Coop would have assigned someone else to be here. At least we're familiar."

"Yes, we are."

I rose from the bed and walked through the rest of the house, stopping when I reached the kitchen. Gran had a habit of littering the outside of the refrigerator with photos. Today they looked different somehow. I leaned in, taking a closer look.

"What is it?" Maddie asked.

I shrugged. "I'm not sure. Some of these photos have been here for years, and it looks like they've been rearranged."

"Huh, that's strange."

I went row by row, checking for any I hadn't noticed before. On the third row, I found what I was looking for—an older photo of a newborn baby.

Maddie reached out, grabbing my shoulder. "Sloane, are you all right? You're shaking."

"He was here, he was in here, in Gran's house."

"Who was here? The killer?"

I nodded.

"How do you know?" she asked.

I removed the picture, staring in disbelief at the playing card stuck behind it—the Ace of Hearts.

Maddie looked at the playing card and then at the photo I held in my hand. She detached the card and flipped it around, reading aloud:

How does it feel to lose the one you love?
How does it feel to never know him?

CHAPTER 39

I need to tell you both something," I said, "and I don't want either of you to get mad."

"Whatever it is, you know you can tell us," Nick said.

"Yeah," Maddie said. "Why would we get mad?"

"Because it's something I should have told you both a long time ago, something no one knows, except for a few people, like Gran."

"Are you referring to the baby in the photo?" Maddie asked. "Who is he?"

"You both know I was married once a long time ago, before I knew either of you."

Maddie shrugged. "Yeah, to that alcoholic loser you dated when you were in high school."

"Logan, yes. I've also told you that when he had too much to drink, he was physically abusive, taking his anger out on me. The night I finally told him I wanted a divorce, he attacked me."

"Yeah," Maddie frowned. "We've seen your scar. I'm so glad you got away from him when you did."

"After I got the restraining order, I moved in with Gran and Gramps, and Logan never dared come after me because he knew if he did, Gramps would have killed him."

"Well, yeah," Maddie said, "your grandpa was a badass FBI agent."

"What does your past with Logan have to do with the photo of the baby?" Nick asked.

It only took a few seconds for him to figure out the answer for himself, and a look of shock to set in.

Maddie looked at Nick and then at me. "What's going on here, guys? What am I missing?"

I took a deep breath. "The baby in this photo is mine. He's my son."

Maddie jerked back, waving a hand in front of her. "What? No! I don't believe it. No way! You've never had any kids. I mean, I thought you said you couldn't have any kids?"

"I can't now. I mean, I couldn't, not after I had him."

The pain and hurt on her face mirrored Nick's. My best friend and my ex-boyfriend, both significant parts of my life, and I'd kept a monumental secret from them.

"So where is your baby?" Maddie said. "And when did you have him?"

"The night I left Logan and filed for divorce, I didn't know I was pregnant. I mean, I suspected I might be, but I wasn't certain."

"When did you find out?"

"The minute Gran took me in, I threw up. A few days later, she bought a pregnancy test, and it was confirmed."

"What did you do?"

"I thought about keeping him at first. I wanted to keep him, and had I known I wouldn't ever have a child again, maybe I would have."

"What made you decide to give him up?"

"Gran kept talking to me about how young I was and about how I'd have to spend the rest of my life trying to keep him a secret. Logan had relatives in Park City. Gran worried Logan would find out and sober up just long enough to convince a judge to give him some kind of custody. Even with Gramps' connections, there was no guarantee I could keep the baby from Logan for his entire life."

"So you decided not to tell him at all?" Maddie asked.

I nodded. "All I wanted to do was to protect the little guy. I didn't want him to grow up to be like his father."

Maddie leaned against the counter, stared at the floor. "I get why you didn't tell him, but why wouldn't you tell me? I'm your best friend."

"I was ashamed, I guess. Both of you have every right to be angry with me. I shouldn't have allowed my fear of reliving the past keep me from telling you the truth."

Nick crossed his arms. "So, where is the boy now?"

"I don't know. It was a closed adoption. Back then most adoptions were. I haven't had any contact with the agency or the parents since I gave him up. Prior to his birth, the agency helped me find a good family."

"Did you meet them, the adoptive family?" Maddie asked.

"Once, right before I gave birth. They were good people. I felt like they would give him a good life."

"Did they know about Logan?"

"I told them he didn't want to be part of the baby's life."

"Even if Logan found out about his son," Nick said, "why wouldn't he just confront you about it? Why go on a killing spree?"

"Yeah," Maddie added. "How can you be sure it's him?"

Because Logan was volatile.

"A couple of years after our divorce, Logan met a girl at a bar, and after three months of knowing her, they married. She was a drifter, claimed to have no home and no family. About six months into the marriage, she found out she was pregnant and didn't tell him. She never wanted kids, and I guess he'd just assumed she would come around. While he was away one weekend, she had an abortion. She made the mistake of telling a girl she had been hanging out with in town. The girl told one of her friends, and that friend told Logan. A couple days after Logan returned, Beth disappeared."

"What do you mean *disappeared*?" Nick asked.

"Logan filed a missing-persons report and showed the local cops a note he claimed Beth had left behind."

"What did the note say?"

"It said she was leaving. She couldn't handle married life and needed to be on her own again. The cops looked into it, but without any family interested in pursuing it, or any evidence to prove she really hadn't just left town, there wasn't a lot they could do. Her body was never found, and no one ever saw her again."

"Are you saying you think he killed her?" Nick asked.

"In my opinion? Yes, that's exactly what he did."

CHAPTER 40

Logan ran a quick errand to the local grocery store, leaving Cordelia zip-tied to an old metal furnace in the bedroom. He'd thought about gagging her before he left but then decided there was no point. The cabin he'd rented was several miles outside of Park City. She could scream for days. No one would hear her.

Back at the cabin, he folded the egg over the cheese, slid the omelette onto a plate, and switched the burner off, staring down at his culinary creation. The egg was a bit crispy on the edges and not entirely intact, but it served its purpose. He'd never been much of a cook, preferring a simple hoagie and a stiff drink to putting forth the effort needed to make a meal for himself, but today he was cooking for two, and he supposed he needed to give her something more than the fast food he'd offered earlier in the day.

He walked down the hall and entered the bedroom, almost turning and walking back out again when he was greeted with an irritating scowl.

"I made you some eggs," he said, "if you're interested."

"It's about time," she spat.

He clipped the zip-ties off of her wrists with a pair of scissors, slid the plate in front of her, and grinned, thinking back to a time over decades earlier when he and Sloane were dating, and he actually cared for the old broad. "You always were a tough old bitch."

She glanced in his direction. "You got that right."

He laughed, and she did too, which he found puzzling. It had been a long time since he'd seen her. It was possible she was losing her marbles in her old age. Then again, he was several marbles short of a handful himself.

She set the plate on her lap, frowning at his choice in silverware. "Is a cheap plastic fork the best you can do?"

"Yep. Don't trust you with a metal one."

"Why not? You're the one holding the gun, aren't you?"

True. But she was intelligent, and he knew better than to underestimate her.

She stabbed at the egg with a fork, stuck a piece in her mouth, and screwed up her face. "Oh, for goodness sake, have you never cooked before?"

He bent over, gripped the corner of the plate, and tugged it toward him. "I could take it back, let you starve."

She snatched it back. "Don't you dare."

"Want a beer to go with it? That's all I have. Well, except for water."

She shrugged. "Sure, why the hell not? You plan on joining me?"

He grinned, mimicking her. "Sure, why the hell not?"

She set the fork down and rubbed her wrists, and he

noticed gashes on both arms where the zip-ties had been. He supposed he should have felt badly for her, but he didn't. He snapped the cap off the beer and held it out.

"I guess I should thank you for your ... well, small sliver of hospitality," she said. "If I can call it that, except you *are* holding me against my will. Are we ever going to talk about why I'm here, or am I supposed to guess?"

He liked the idea.

"Go ahead. Guess."

"This isn't a game, Logan. Not to me, it isn't. Does this have anything to do with Sloane? I mean, you haven't seen her in what, twenty-something years?"

"It has everything to do with her."

"Can you tell me why?"

"She took something from me."

She raised a brow. "I seem to recall you taking a lot more from her when you two were together. Mmm?"

His temper flared. She was testing him with her sarcastic remarks, seeing how far she could go. He'd entertain it, but not for long. "Did you know about him?"

"You'll need to tell me who we're talking about first."

"The baby. Our baby. My son."

He stared at her, waiting for a reaction. She must have known about the baby. She had to know, and yet she met his gaze and didn't even blink.

"She didn't want to give him away, you know. She wanted to keep him."

Through gritted teeth, he said, "Then why did she?"

"It wasn't my doing, and it wasn't Sloane's either. It was her grandfather's idea. It was the only way he'd allow her to stay in his house after you two split up. And you remember how he was at getting what he wanted, don't you?"

He remembered all right, all too well. He'd always hated Sloane's grandfather and his "holier than thou" attitude. But was Cordelia telling the truth? The old man was dead. There was no way to know if she was lying or not. "She still had a choice, and she made it. He was my baby too. She should have asked me."

"How do you know about the child, Logan? Sloane doesn't even know where he is. She tried finding him once and couldn't. Did he come looking for you?"

"Maybe."

"He must be graduated from high school now. I've always wondered how he turned out, what he was like, what he looked like."

Logan dug into his back pocket and pulled out a photo. He showed it to her.

"Where was this taken?" she asked.

"My house, after he came to see me."

"He's very handsome. I see you in him. Sloane too."

Now she was just trying to appease him. It wouldn't work. He shoved the photo back into his pocket and stood, holding out a hand for the plate. "Going to have to tie you back up again."

"I don't understand why any of this is necessary. Why won't you tell me?"

"You'll see, soon enough," he grunted.

"Logan, there must be a way for us to—"

"Stop talking, or I'll gag you too."

She made a face like it didn't matter one way or the other. "Do what you have to do."

"Don't you care about what happens to you?"

"Do I look like I care?"

He almost laughed again, but didn't.

"Will you tell me the boy's name at least?" she asked.

He pulled two new zip-ties out of his front pocket and fastened her hands back together without answering the question. Walking out of the room, he glanced over his shoulder before slipping out of sight. Her eyes were fixed on him, narrow and fierce, like she would stab him right through the heart if she could.

He didn't blame her, and he hated to admit he actually enjoyed her company. It was almost a shame she had to die.

CHAPTER 41

I stepped out of the shower and noticed my cell phone was lit up. I grabbed it off the counter and took a look. I'd received two photo messages from an unknown number. The first was an Ace of Hearts. The second was Gran, sitting on a hardwood floor, her wrists tied to the slats of a heater, painful to see.

Me: *Logan, is this you?*

Him: *Bravo.*

Me: *What do you want?*

Him: *You know.*

Me: *Me?*

Him: *Yes.*

Me: *Why?*

I waited. He didn't reply.

Me: *Please, don't hurt Gran.*

Him: *What happens to her is up to you.*

Me: *Tell me what I need to do.*

Him: *Are you alone?*

Me: *Yes.*

Him: *How do I know you're not lying?*

I snapped a photo of myself standing in the bathroom dressed in nothing but a towel and sent it to him. It was the last thing I wanted to do, but I couldn't think of a better alternative.

Me: *Did you get the photo?*

Him: *Yeah, doesn't mean you're alone.*

Me: *Stop wasting my time and tell me what you want me to do!*

One minute passed, then two. When he still hadn't written back after three, I feared I'd angered him.

Me: *Logan, please. I'll do anything.*

Him: *Meet me at the back of the Gatsby Automotive parking lot. One hour. Come alone. If anyone is with you, you'll never see Cordelia again.*

Me: *I need more time. The chief of police is here, a detective, and two officers are parked outside. I can't just walk out unnoticed.*

It was true, and they had all gathered together at Maddie's place to keep an eye on me, and to plan their next move.

Him: *If you want her to live, you'll find a way. See you soon.*

I clicked my phone off, slipped into the bedroom, and got dressed. The men were in the living room, talking amongst themselves. I glanced out the window. Two officers sat in a car on the street. If I tried going out my window, they'd see me. It was too risky. My best bet was to exit through the window on the side of the house, and that meant going through Maddie's office. Problem was, I couldn't get to it without going through the living room, where Coop and Nick were sitting.

I strolled down the hallway, doing my best to act like everything was fine, and it worked until I saw Maddie eyeing me when I walked by. One look at my face and she tilted her head to the side, aware something was up. I tried giving her a nonverbal sign to keep quiet, but it didn't work. When she opened her mouth to ask me what I was doing, and both men in the living room turned toward me, I knew I had to come up with something, and fast.

"Maddie, I need to look up something on your office computer. Can you come help me?"

I managed to appease her, and she slid off of the sofa and followed me into the office.

"Shut the door," I whispered.

"Why?"

"Just shut it, okay?"

"What's going on, Sloane?"

"I have to leave without being noticed, and I need you to keep quiet about it."

"I don't get it. What happened?"

"Logan texted me. I was right. He's the killer. He's behind everything that's happened."

I showed her the messages.

"Whatever you're planning on doing right now, and whatever he has asked you to do, it's not a good idea. Don't do it."

"I have to, Maddie. If I don't give him what he wants, Gran will die."

"If you walk into his trap, you both will."

"It's a risk I'm willing to take, and I don't have time to sit here and argue about it. Help me or don't. Either way, I'm going."

I lifted the office window.

She placed both hands on her hips, and then pointed to a chair in front of her desk. "Wear my jacket, at least. It's freezing out there. Do you have your gun?"

I pulled up my shirt, showed it to her.

"If you expect me to let you walk out of here without me saying anything to anyone, you need to tell me where you're going first," she said.

"We're meeting at Gatsby Automotive in …" I glanced at the clock on the wall. "Forty-five minutes."

"And then what happens?"

"I have no idea." I handed her my phone. "Wait twenty minutes, then give this to Coop and tell him where I went."

"No way, you should keep it."

"Just give it to him, okay? Let me take yours."

She reached into her pocket, handed it to me. "How are you getting to Gatsby's? You'll never make it on time on foot."

"I requested an Uber. He's picking me up on the next street in a few minutes. I need to go, right now."

Worried, she wrapped her arms around me. "I don't like this. I don't want you to go."

I climbed out the window. "I'm not saying I'll be able to reason with him, but I need to try at least. We have history. I'll find a way to get through to him if I can. I've been in worse situations than this one, and I'm still here. Gran's life is on the line. I'm not letting anyone else die because of me."

She sighed. "Fine. What can I do?"

"Distract the cops outside so I can get out of here."

She nodded. "I'm on it. Please, be safe."

CHAPTER 42

Logan sized me up and down. "You look a lot different."

"So do you," I said.

And he did—tired and old, wasted, the years of drinking taking a toll in the form of lines and creases on his face, a face that in our youth had once been more handsome than all the rest.

He leaned against a black sedan, tapping on the side of his gun with a finger. "Why did you cut your hair off?"

I shrugged. "Why does it matter? It's my hair. I needed a change."

"Yeah, well, it looked better longer."

I focused the conversation on what mattered. "Where is Gran? Is she here?"

"She's back at the cabin. It isn't far."

The cabin. I guessed it was far enough.

"Is she alive?"

"For now. Hold your hands out in front of you."

"Why?"

He shoved me against the car. "Shut up, and don't ask questions."

I pressed my arms together, pushing them in his direction. He laced a zip-tie around my wrists, pulling it so tight I winced.

"Now what?" I asked.

"Now you get in the car." He escorted me to the passenger side and opened the door. "Hang on. Don't get in yet."

"Why not?"

He reached inside my pockets, felt beneath my clothes, finding my gun, which I expected. He stuck it in his coat pocket. "Nice try. Where did you hide your cell phone?"

Maddie's phone was a bit trickier, and tiny, one of the smallest I'd ever seen. I'd tucked it inside one of the cups of my bra. As long as I didn't have to bend over or move too much, I assumed there was about a fifty-fifty chance it would remain in place, and if I could keep it on, I could be tracked.

"I don't have my phone. I didn't bring it with me."

He smacked my head against the side of the car—hard. "Liar! Where is it?"

A car turned down the street, shifting Logan's attention. He grabbed me, jerking the two of us out of sight. He pressed the barrel of the gun against my cheek. "Who did you tell? Who knows you're here? I'll kill you right here, right now, if you lie to me again."

"No one knows I'm here. You're being paranoid."

He pressed his other hand against my throat and squeezed. "Stop lying to me! Who's in the car?"

Gagging and struggling for breath, I said, "I ... don't ... know ... Logan. I swear."

The car drove past the automotive shop and kept on going, turning into a residential neighborhood.

"See, I told you."

I thought about Maddie, guessing she wouldn't keep quiet long. If I wanted to get to Gran, we needed to go. Now. "I gave you what you wanted. I came. I want to see Gran."

He jerked on the door handle and shoved me inside. "Oh, don't worry. You will."

CHAPTER 43

A short time later, we followed a dirt road to a small cabin in a wooded area beyond Park City. It was perfect—desolate and run down. The kind of place where a person could be taken and never found. Logan walked me into the house and down the hall to the bedroom.

"You get one minute," he said. "Don't do anything stupid."

He stepped out of the room, but I knew he was probably just around the corner, didn't go far, leaving me to assume he was standing around the corner, listening in on the conversation.

"Gran!" I dropped down in front of her, wishing my wrists were free so I could give her the kind of loving embrace we both needed. "Are you all right?"

She looked fatigued and weak, but tenacious. He hadn't broken her spirit. She looked both happy and sad to see me at the same time. "You shouldn't be here."

"I had to come."

"No good can come of it. He knows about the boy. That's what this is all about."

"I know. He killed Shelby."

"What? I don't understand. Why?"

"And Cade is in the hospital too. Logan shot him in the head."

Gran tipped her head, motioning me to come closer.

"You need to get out of here if you can," she whispered. "If he killed them, he'll kill you too."

"Not without you. I think I can reason with him."

"I don't think so, Sloane. Have you looked at him—really looked at him? There's something there, in his eyes, a different man than before, and he was never a good man to begin with."

She was right. The moment I laid eyes on him, I'd seen the snap.

Logan entered the room with a wide grin on his face. He had what he wanted just the way he wanted it, and he was satisfied. "Time's up, ladies."

Hoping to appeal to him, I questioned why I couldn't remain with Gran longer. "I'm here, Logan, just like you wanted. No one knows where to find me. Can't I have more time?"

"Sure, you can. I'll give you the same amount of time you gave me with my son."

And before I could stop him, he aimed the gun at Gran and fired.

CHAPTER 44

The bullet struck Gran in the chest. I lunged toward her, but before I reached her, Logan was on top of me, grabbing the back of my shirt. He shoved me out of the way and stood over Gran's body. "Did you really think I believed your story about your husband being the one to decide to give my son away? You're a shrewd, rigid woman. Always have been. It was you. It was you all along."

Gran's breath was slow and shallow. She gasped for air, struggling for even the smallest breath. It was then I realized why he had kept her alive. It was the ultimate payback, bringing me there so I could watch her die, so I could suffer just as he had suffered.

He raised the gun again, this time to her head. I crawled toward her, throwing my body on top of hers. He turned to me, laughing. "There's nothing you can do for her now, but hey, maybe you're right. Maybe I shouldn't make it easy on her. Let her bleed for a while. Let her writhe in pain."

He yanked me out of the bedroom and into the living room, hurling me onto the couch. "I think it's time we talk about our son, don't you?"

"What about him?"

"So you don't deny it?"

"Why would I deny it now? What would be the point?"

"Want to know his name?"

The cards, the quotes—it was clear to me now. "Is his name Ace?"

He clapped his hands. "Well, well, gold star for the little sleuth."

"How did you find out about him?"

"The woman who raised him died last month. She had breast cancer. Before her death, she called him into her room and said she had something to tell him. He was raised to believe she was his mother, his bio mother, and before she passed she thought he deserved to know the truth. She gave him the name of his real parents. All she had was our names, but it turns out, with all the technology out there nowadays, that's all he needed to seek us out."

"It's not possible. How would she know what our names are? It was a closed adoption. The paperwork was sealed."

"The caseworker at the agency was good friends with the adoptive mother. The caseworker thought Ace was a good match for the woman because she knew you'd never try to take him back. She also knew I'd never step in because I didn't know he existed."

His words shocked me. "His adoptive parents knew who we were all these years and kept it quiet."

"After the woman died, he found out where I lived and drove out to California to meet me."

"I don't understand. This is the first I'm hearing about it. He's done nothing to reach out to me. Why?"

"Guess you could say it was a lucky roll of the dice. He found me first, and said he wondered what I was like."

What he was like was a living, breathing nightmare, one from which I thought I could protect my son.

"After he saw you, he could have reached out to me. Why hasn't he?"

"Because I told him the truth about you."

"What *truth*?"

"I told him what you did, that I never knew he existed. I said you didn't want him. You gave him up without even giving me a chance. I never had a say in the matter. You decided what was best for the both of us and did it without my permission."

"That's not true; that's not what happened. You weren't around. You don't know how hard it was for me at the time."

"Hard for *you*?"

He slammed his fist into my jaw, and I reeled back, my head smacking against the wall behind me. The copper taste of blood filled my mouth.

"There's no point in lying now," he said. "It's just you and me here. There's no one around to judge you for what you've done. No one except me."

"Are you saying you became so enraged over me hiding him from you that you decided to lash out, shooting anyone who has ever mattered to me?"

He hung his head. "No. It's not that simple."

"Explain, because it seems simple enough to me."

"He's *dead*, Sloane. My boy is dead."

Dead? No. He couldn't be.

"How? You said you just saw him?"

"I did. We met, hung out for the day, and before he left, I invited him back. He said he'd come out again the following weekend. The next weekend came and went and he never showed. I called. He didn't answer. I texted. He didn't reply. I thought maybe I had the weekend wrong, and maybe he meant to come in two weekends, but when that weekend went by and I still hadn't heard from him, I decided he must have changed his mind. I wasn't about to lose my son a second time. I drove to Idaho to the farm where he was living."

"And did you find him?"

"I found his family, his *fake* family. The man who raised Ace had no idea he'd been in contact with me. He didn't even know his wife had told the boy the truth about who his parents were."

"And Ace, where was he?"

Logan shook his head. "Already dead. He had told the man he was going out of town for the weekend, which means he was coming to see me just like he said he would. About an hour into the drive, a car swerved into his lane, some stupid broad looking at a text message on her cell phone. She slammed into him. He didn't have his seatbelt on. Went right through the windshield."

"I … I don't know what to … I can't believe—"

His anger surged. "Oh, yeah? Which part, Sloane? Which part can't you believe? Because you know which part I'm struggling with the most?"

I didn't even need to ask. I already knew. After Ace's death, Logan must have decided if I hadn't kept our son from him, he'd still be alive, and the course of events wouldn't have played out the way they did.

"You see now?" Logan seethed. "You destroyed my family, so I destroyed yours."

"Shelby was innocent, Logan. They were all innocent. If you wanted to kill someone, you should have just killed me."

Except he couldn't. His rage festered until he was blinded by it. He wanted me to suffer as he'd suffered.

"I came to find you after it happened, and wouldn't you know, I discovered you had a new family now. You ditched our kid and then went and raised another one with someone else. That girl, Shelby, she wasn't even your blood."

"I didn't raise Shelby. She was a teenager when I met her."

"We could have had a happy life, the three of us. You ruined it. You ruined it all."

"A happy life!" Wrists still bound, I managed to raise my shirt just enough to show him the scar he'd inflicted so long ago. "Remember *this*? Remember the man you were then, the man you *still* are now? I would rather my son leave this life knowing he was loved than to have spent a single moment with the man you really are!"

He grabbed the collar of my shirt, yanking me forward, our faces pressed against each other. The cell phone tucked beneath my bra came tumbling out, clanking on the floor.

Eyes wide, Logan snatched it. "You kidding me?"

I snapped my foot back, sweeping it through the air, smashing it into the side of his face. It was one of the moves I'd come to master in jiu jitsu over the years, the martial art I learned after I had left Logan, vowing never to be helpless again. He may have been big and tough, built like a Mack truck, but I'd struck him with all the force I had, jolting him long enough for me to get to steady myself.

For a split second I thought about running to the front door, but I couldn't, not before I knew whether Gran was still alive or not. I raced to the bedroom, slammed the door, and locked it. I dropped down in front of her, gripping her body in my hands. I shook her, but there was no movement, and her eyes remained closed.

"Gran? Gran! Can you hear me? Please! We don't have much time."

Outside Logan kicked at the door, but it was old and thick, made of solid wood. He wouldn't get in easily. I guided my shaky hand toward Gran's neck, feeling for a pulse. It was there, but it was weak.

Enraged, Logan doubled his efforts, kicking at the door and shooting at it with his gun at the same time. He was almost inside. I searched the room for a weapon, any weapon, anything I could use to protect myself. My options were limited to a vase on the dresser. I snatched it, stood behind the door, and waited.

Chunks of wood spit into the room as Logan forged a hole in the door big enough to shove his hand through. He reached his hand inside, and I smashed it with my foot. He pulled his hand back, howling in pain. Undeterred, he grabbed for the door handle again, and this time he got it unlocked.

"You're a dead woman, Sloane," he taunted.

I steadied the vase in my hand, hoping it wasn't the end.

My end.

A familiar voice thundered down the hallway, a voice that had never brought me as much happiness as it did in that moment.

"Put the gun down, Logan," Coop said.

"Not a chance."

Two shots rang out, nearly simultaneously. I yanked the door open, finding Coop on the other side, curled over Logan, smiling.

Coop glanced at me, nodded, and then looked at Logan and said, "Enjoy hell, you son of a bitch."

CHAPTER 45

Several months later, I watched the physical therapist offer positive reinforcement as he worked through Cade's daily two-hour routine. What started as him learning to walk again by pushing a shopping cart from one side of the room to the other had evolved into Cade walking the same distance on his own with nothing more than a slight limp. He wasn't fast, but he was resolute, bouncing back in a way his doctors considered a miracle.

He had almost no recollection of the day of the shooting, or of the funeral, or of the first two weeks he'd spent at the hospital before being transferred to a specialist in Utah. I suppose it was a bit of a blessing in disguise, to erase the bad and replace it with good. He was alive, and he was thriving.

One event I couldn't erase was Cade's memory of what had happened to Shelby. Explaining why it happened proved more difficult than I'd ever imagined, and because he was still recovering, his doctor was worried he'd have a setback and advised me to hold off at first. But waiting wasn't an option when it came to Cade. He'd always been a straight shooter, and one night as we had just sat down to dinner, he'd placed a hand over mine and said, "I need you to tell me, no matter how hard it is."

It was the defining moment in our relationship, and I had convinced myself that once I told him the truth, we would be over. After all, how could any man be expected to stay with the person responsible for the death of his only child?

"It's my fault," I'd said. "Shelby died because of me."

He'd taken a sip of beer, leaned back in the chair, and squinted at me. "I don't see how that's true, but go on."

I hadn't wanted to go on, but I did, keeping my eye on him as I spoke about my son and Logan, and the rage that drove Logan to do what he did. Jaw clenched, and eyes filled with a mixture of anger and sorrow, he'd sat quiet and still, until the silence became more than I could bear.

"If you don't want to be with me anymore, I understand," I had said. "I don't know what I'd do if the same thing happened to—"

"Sloane."

"Yeah?"

"Stop beatin' yourself up. I'm still here, sittin' right in front of you."

"Things aren't the same now though, Cade. I don't see how they ever will be. I feel like you'll always look at me and be reminded of what you lost."

"You're right. They're not the same, and I'm not gonna lie and say they ever will be, but the only way we'll get through this now is together. No runnin' away this time. You hear me?"

I looked at him solidly in that moment and nodded, feeling undeserving of such an understanding, tolerant man. I had always remained by his side, and though our life had been forever altered, over the ensuing months, we would learn how to bond over the tragedy and to lean on each other for support during the tough days ahead.

Things were good now—different, but good.

The physical therapist finished up for the day and said goodbye. Cade reached out, running a hand through my hair.

"Hey, you went away for a minute," he said. "What were you thinkin' about?"

"Nothing much," I said. "What would you like to do today?"

"I was thinkin' we should invite Maddie and Cordelia to visit. You've been so busy takin' care of me all these months, you haven't had time for anyone else."

I shrugged. "I can give them a call, see when they have time to drive over for a couple days."

Maddie's head popped out from behind the corner. "No need. We're already here!"

Gran and Maddie walked toward me.

"When did you get here?" I asked.

"This morning," Gran said. "Cade stowed us away for a bit, so we could surprise you."

"I can't believe it," I said. "How long are you staying?"

Maddie thumbed toward Cade. "Ahh … maybe you should ask him."

When I turned back around, the ring box was extended for a second time.

"Let's try this again," Cade said. "What do you say?"

I could tell he'd planned to go on, but there was nothing more he needed to say that hadn't already been said. I dropped to my knees, clasped his hands in mine and said, "Yes, Cade. I say yes."

THE END

About Cheryl Bradshaw

Cheryl Bradshaw is a New York Times and USA Today bestselling author. She currently has two series: Sloane Monroe mystery/thriller series and the Addison Lockhart paranormal suspense series. Stranger in Town (Sloane Monroe series #4) was a 2013 Shamus Award finalist for Best PI Novel of the Year, and I Have a Secret (Sloane Monroe series #3) was a 2013 eFestival of Words winner for best thriller novel.

Enjoy the Story?

If you enjoyed *Gone Daddy Gone*, you can show your appreciation by leaving a review on Amazon, Barnes & Noble, iBooks, or in the Kobo Store. And, if you do write a review, please be sure to email Cheryl via her website http://www.cherylbradshaw.com so she can express her gratitude.

Books by Cheryl Bradshaw

Sloane Monroe Series
Black Diamond Death
Murder in Mind
I Have a Secret
Stranger in Town
Bed of Bones
Flirting With Danger (Novella)
Hush Now Baby
Dead of Night (Novella)
Gone Daddy Gone

Addison Lockhart Series
Grayson Manor Haunting
Rosecliff Manor Haunting

Maisie Fezziwig Series
Hickory Dickory Dead

Till Death do us Part Short Story Series
Whispers of Murder
Echoes of Murder

Stand-Alone Novels
Eye for Revenge
The Devil Died at Midnight